BLUE
DANUBE

An imprint of Somerset Books, Budapest
Distributed by Blue Guides Limited of London
Distributed in the USA by WW Norton & Company, Inc.
500 Fifth Avenue, New York, NY 10110.

Translated from the Hungarian: *Milolu* (1949)
English translation © Thomas Sneddon 2021
Afterword © Thomas Barcsay 2021.

ISBN 978-1-905131-89-1

Cover: Detail from an Italian travel poster, c. 1930.
Map by Dimap Bt.

Every effort has been made to contact the copyright owners
of material reproduced in this book.
We would be pleased to hear from any copyright owners
we have been unable to reach.

Printed and bound in Great Britain by TJ Books.

 somersetbooks.com/bluedanube

The Remarkable
Mrs ANDERSON

Miklós Bánffy

Translated from the Hungarian
by Thomas Sneddon
with an Afterword by Thomas Barcsay

BLUE DANUBE

I

Calamity!

On the 14th of December, a painting by Leonardo da Vinci—and not some careless, half-finished sketch, but a genuine masterpiece—was stolen from the Budapest Fine Arts Museum. Who would venture to calculate the worth of such a treasure? So few paintings by that incomparable genius remain, but this one is particularly special: the same figure who later represents Jesus in the *Last Supper* is also depicted here, and experts surmise that the master was perfecting his technique, working from the original model and preparing for the great fresco to come. The *Last Supper*, alas, is badly faded, so this is the only work in which we can see that face in glorious, living colour. None of the Museum's other treasures, not even the Raphael *Madonna and Child*, or Giorgione's self-portrait, quite compare to the monumental value of this work.

Stolen!

The Museum was closed to the public at the time. With winter approaching, it had been decided that certain necessary maintenance work could no longer be put off. Plasterers, decorators and their assistants were brought in to work in the central hall, smoothing and repainting the rather careworn façades and scraping off the sooty grime which had percolated in from the nearby railway line. One of the radiators in the Renaissance gallery on the first floor leaked, and a plumber was busy ripping out the old heating pipes. These all had to be taken out and brought down to the outdoor courtyard to be soldered, since naked flames are prohibited in the building itself. Everything was to be finished within a week.

The artisans undertaking this work were all professionals with long-established ties to the Museum. The main entrance was of course locked, so they were admitted though the side door which opens onto Aréna Street, and after the last man left in the evening the night porter locked this door too.

It was eight o'clock in the morning and all the tradesmen had already been at work for half an hour or so when the doorbell rang. The porter opened the door a few inches. Before him stood a tall, thin young man in an old set of paint-spattered overalls, tufts of blonde hair sticking out from beneath a cloth cap. Under his arm was a thick wad of newspaper tied up with brown string, while in his hand he clutched three little pouches of powdered paint.

'I'm Mr Fodor's assistant,' he said. 'I was just at the stores, getting him fresh paint and lining paper.'

The porter let him in.

Reaching the first public gallery, the porter unlocked the steel-and-glass door and ushered the young man through.

'Right, then right again at the end of the corridor,' he said, then locked the door behind him.

The young man headed obediently right, and the porter watched him until he disappeared behind the columns and free-standing sculptures.

Barely fifteen minutes later he was back. Frowning, the porter opened the door.

'What's this about? You finished already or what?'

The young man gestured ruefully at the thick wad of newspaper still clasped under his arm.

'The boss needs plain paper, not this newsprint. I'm to take this back and get it changed.'

His manner was so convincing and the explanation so straightforward, that the porter never thought to doubt him. He led the young man through to the street door and let him out.

By lunchtime the radiator had at last been safely removed from its mountings. The plumber and the security guard lifted it up and set off towards the service stairs. Their route took them through the little room adjoining the main Renaissance gallery, where small-sized works are arranged according to school or period. Rounding the corner and entering this smaller room, a visitor was usually confronted by Leonardo's *Head of Christ*, the only painting on the far wall. Encased in a gold frame, which was itself a masterpiece of considerable value, it hung against a wallpaper of green velvet.

The cast-iron radiator was exceedingly heavy, and the two men agreed to stop for a quick breather. Setting the radiator down and wiping his brow, the guard happened to glance at the far wall.

The gold frame was empty!

The painting had been there when he passed by first thing in the morning and now it was gone! The guard gaped dumbfounded at the empty space. He tried to speak, but words would not come. At last he managed a strangled croak.

'Quick!'

He and the plumber charged through the galleries until they reached the top of the stairs, then the guard turned and locked the heavy wooden doors with both keys.

'Don't move! Don't bloody move from this spot whatever you do! Lord, what a mess! I'm going to get help, but don't move!'

He bounded down the stairs four at a time and burst into the Director's office with the terrible news. The Director immediately phoned the police, informing them that a serious crime had been committed. A fleet of police cars soon roared up, sirens wailing, and the official investigation began.

It was soon established that the men actually working on the Museum refurbishment were innocent. The only credible suspect was the tall, thin young man who had arrived a little later than the others in a set of painter's overalls. There was indeed a Mr Fodor employed by the Museum, but he had sent no one for paint or paper, and both his apprentice and his assistant had been with him all morning. The plumber, likewise, had been in the guard's sight at all times.

This was a fresh blow; the painting had been gone for hours! The thin young man had left before half past eight and it was now one in the afternoon. That meant more than four hours had elapsed: more than enough time for the thieves to reach Czechoslovakia or even Austria. The Vienna Express, after all, left Budapest at precisely nine. The police considered it more likely, however, that the thieves would travel by car: border checks were always more perfunctory at road crossings than on the train.

Still, every possible measure was put in place at once, and the police department's best detectives were assigned to the case. Phone calls were made to every border checkpoint, ordering the guards to conduct exhaustive searches of all luggage. If they found anything matching the description of the stolen painting they were immediately to detain whoever carried it. A parallel investigation also sought to determine the identity of the man in the paint-spattered overalls. Their only clues were the three little pouches of powdered paint which had been found in the cast gallery. There was no packaging of any kind, however, and inquiries at paint supply shops across the city turned up nobody who had bought powdered paint on the morning of the fourteenth. Either the thief or an accomplice must have purchased it earlier, in preparation for the heist.

The Director immediately informed the Home Secretary of what had happened, and the Home Secretary ordered them to keep everything under wraps while the investigation was underway. It was, in fact, to remain a secret unless there was some hope that publicity would lead to its recovery; it would do enormous harm to the reputation of the Museum —and the nation—if an audacious daylight robbery of one of Hungary's most highly prized treasures became common knowledge.

'They'd bring you down, my dear fellow,' the Home Secretary said. 'They might even bring *me* down! These opposition politicians are vultures, you know, and they'd happily use a case like this against me, though as you know I have as little to do with the whole affair as a new-born child! The truth is, I wouldn't lay any blame on the Museum either. You can't even fault the security guard who failed to lock the service stairs behind him, since he felt absolutely certain that no intruders would enter the building. No, I won't have anyone charged, not even the porter who let the scoundrel in. God help us, the opposition would have a field day!'

So for the time being only some of the Museum staff, the police investigators and a few government officials knew of what had happened. Nobody else. A week later the Museum reopened, with the Italian gallery remaining closed for reasons of 'routine maintenance'.

The investigation continued, but things seemed to be going nowhere. Then, on the sixteenth of January, a most peculiar thing happened. Around ten o'clock in the morning an unfamiliar voice called the Director's office from an unknown location.

'Am I speaking to the Director in person?'

'You are. Who is this?'

'I am calling to inform you that the picture you are searching for is in a dark grey travelling trunk, which was deposited in the luggage room of Keleti railway station this morning. Go at once and you'll find it there…' The speaker hung up.

Within ten minutes the Director and a police detective were weaving through traffic in a speeding taxi, heading for Keleti Station. The detective showed his badge to the luggage room attendant, who obediently unlocked the storeroom. Only one item matched the description given on the phone: a rather battered-looking travelling trunk of a very old make. It opened easily and there was only one object inside. A bulky, rectangular frame wrapped in a linen cloth, with wooden blocks at the corners to hold it in place.

The Director immediately lifted it from the trunk and tore off the linen covering.

'Yes!' he cried, perspiration beading on his forehead. 'Yes! We've got it, thank God! I thought this business was going to put me in an early grave!'

The detective was already questioning the luggage attendant.

'Who left this here? When? What did he look like?'

The attendant could only say with certainty when it had been dropped off. It had been early that same morning, at around the time the Kassa Express pulled in. The Trieste and Vienna expresses both left within half an hour of its arrival, he explained, so it was always the busiest period in the luggage room and today had been no exception. He could no longer remember precisely who had left it.

'It wasn't a lanky blonde man?' the detective asked.

The luggage attendant frowned and blinked.

'Could've been… The truth is, I've no idea. If you were to press me I'd more likely say he was a sort of darker-haired chap, but I really can't say for sure…'

That was relatively unimportant, though; the main thing was that they had the picture back! There was of course wild rejoicing when the Director returned to the Museum. The empty gold frame was brought down to his office, as he wanted to restore this treasure to its rightful place with his own hands. First, however, he called the Home Secretary to pass on the good news.

'Well thank Heaven for that,' the Home Secretary exhaled. 'That's a weight off my mind. Those animals in the opposition would have loved to use this picture business against me. They'd have relished it! Listen, all's well that ends well and all that, but all the same, I want you to keep this affair under your hat. They'd be sure to blame it on the police, and from there it's only a short step to the Home Office. Even the Ministry of Transport could be in trouble, since the picture was in their charge when it was found. We can't have those jackals saying stolen goods were being held on public property when they were discovered! No, not a word of this to anyone!'

'I quite understand, sir. It will be just as you say. Not a word.'

'Tell me, my old friend, when will you be returning it to display?'

'I'm not entirely sure. This evening, I suppose, after closing.'

'You couldn't make it a little earlier? I'd like to be there in person.'

'Certainly, sir, just as you like. If it suits you we could put it up together at three or four in the afternoon.'

'Splendid! I'll be over by half past three at the latest.'

The Home Secretary's presence lent to the event the air almost of a state ceremony. All the Museum functionaries and guards were there, as were the picture restorers and their apprentices. Old Behr, in retirement after a lifetime of service as the Museum's chief restoration specialist, came in for the event.

Two attendants opened the great front doors for the Home Secretary, who was preceded by two men bearing the Leonardo aloft like a holy icon. The Museum Director fell in next to the Home Secretary and everyone else formed a procession behind them. They made their way up to the first floor, where the painting was hung once more in its accustomed place on the wall. The Home Secretary judged this an opportune moment to say a few words, and so the audience was graced with his warm, mellow baritone—the gift to which he primarily owed his high office. He spoke of duty, and of the grave responsibilities entailed by public service. On the other hand, he went on, the government understood that these responsibilities were collective, rather than individual. The situation was not to be viewed simply as an isolated occurrence—which in this case might suggest negligence—but in a broader context which (he cast a significant glance at the porter) took into consideration a man's years of faultless and dedicated service. He closed by exhorting them all to perform their appointed tasks more diligently than ever, while he would continue to do everything in his power to defend the Museum and its employees.

The Director thanked the Home Secretary for his wise and apposite remarks, then undertook on behalf of the entire staff to work with greater zeal than ever to guard the Museum's treasures, so that future generations could profit from their beauty and splendour. This gave him an opportunity to talk about the painting itself—a subject on which he was eager to demonstrate his expertise. All the more so since he did not, in fact, have a reputation as a knowledgeable connoisseur. After much intriguing he had succeeded in ousting his predecessor—an art historian of considerable European standing—and now at last he had an opportunity to show that he could fill the old man's shoes. He began by saying what anyone looking at the painting could see. The canvas was mounted on wooden boards which, on the reverse, had been painted in a deep scarlet known in the business as English Red. The painting depicted the head of Christ and, just as in the *Last Supper*, he was shown with a thin, wispy beard. Here, however, everything was much clearer and more vivid than in the *Last Supper*, which is, of course, in famously poor condition. The neck was only roughly sketched, while the shoulders were barely suggested with a line or two. The faint blue in the background was, he said, only applied directly around the head. The rest was left plain.

'From this we may infer that Leonardo saw the painting before us as a kind of preparatory work, which in a certain sense makes it even more interesting; while we are entirely justified in considering it a finished piece, still we are able to follow the line of his draughtsmanship as though that great master had laid down his brush just yesterday.' Smiling wistfully, he shook his head and—struck by the aptness of his own image—repeated himself. 'As if it were only yesterday...'

The unfortunate Director little guessed how right he was.

The gathering ended with a hearty round of applause for the Home Secretary, then everyone made their way downstairs. Only old Behr lingered. Taking out the strong magnifying glass he always carried in his pocket, he went over to the painting and began examining it. Someone soon called out that they were locking up, so he too went downstairs.

He went back the next Monday, a day when the Museum is always closed, and asked his former apprentice—now the head restoration specialist—to join him.

At first Behr merely made idle conversation, looking around the old familiar space and asking his former colleague what he was working on these days. They looked at the painting currently being restored and the old man offered some advice. Then he asked a seemingly offhand question.

'By the way, you haven't taken a look at the Leonardo since it was returned?'

'Only a quick check. I haven't had time to look it over properly.'

'I always told you, you've got to make a thorough examination of every returning artwork as soon as it arrives, even when it was just out on loan at a very reputable museum or exhibition. It needs to be checked from top to bottom; there might be minor damage, slackened canvas, anything. In this case it's more vital than ever; we don't even know where it was for a month.'

'You're right, I should have examined it already. We can go over it together. I'll fetch it, and meet you in the workshop.'

A few minutes later the painting was in old Behr's hands. He held it very close to his face, almost as though sniffing it, then turned it around to examine the reverse, painted in

English Red to seal the boards against damp. The old man looked at it for a long time, then set it down and lifted his magnifying glass. He peered through it at a tiny patch of unpainted wood in the corner.

'Strange,' he said, shaking his head. 'Very strange.'

He stood thinking for a moment, then turned to his former apprentice.

'Bring down the catalogue, would you? Let's see what exactly is recorded.'

It was some time before the younger man returned, and as he waited Behr continued to frown and shake his head. At last he lifted a palette knife and nicked off a tiny flake of paint from the backboard, placing it in the middle of a scrap of paper and folding it neatly.

The catalogue contained a very precise description, and measurements had been taken to the millimetre: 44.7 centimetres high and 35.1 broad.

'Pass me the measuring tape.'

Behr measured the height and width of the painting on the table.

'Just a small discrepancy. I make this one 44.6 by 34.9, but that sort of slight difference comes up all the time, depending on precisely what points you measure from, or if you count right to the end of the board or just to the end of the flat surface. There's more, though; here on the front, where the wood is meant to be untreated, something seems unnatural about the colour. It's as though someone used oil or wax to darken it artificially. See here? That reddish area at the bottom is like the leftover sediment from a wash. There's something funny about the back, too: I have a suspicion someone used a siccative to dry the paint quickly. The cracks and lesions in the wood—there's something not quite right about them. That's why I flaked off this little scrap of paint; see? I want you to run a chemical analysis of it.'

'But surely you don't mean…? Are you really saying it could be a forgery?'

'I can't say for sure, but it certainly isn't impossible. The red on the back looks somehow duller than I remember, and the plaster grounding seems coated in a very thin, transparent layer; that might be to make it easier to photograph.'

'But—a forgery? That would be… Dear God, I mean, a disaster! Criminal!'

'Undoubtedly. Still, we still can't say anything definite. If fact, we shouldn't even voice our suspicions until we're satisfied one way or the other. The deciding factor is the drying agent. If we can prove the wood has been dried artificially then we'll know for sure. The old masters had drying agents of their own, of course, for when they were in a great hurry, but they always caused the paint to start flaking off before long, whereas this Leonardo was—is—in almost perfect condition.'

'But why would anyone go to the trouble of making such a perfect forgery? Why make us believe we have the painting back?'

Behr smiled. 'I can think of plenty of reasons. If we think we have the original then we won't watch the foreign art markets so closely. They say the border guards have already relaxed their searches and the police departments in Western capitals will have been told that the picture is back in our possession. That means the gang that stole it can sell it more openly and find a wealthier buyer. Still, there's no point speculating until we know what we're dealing with. In any case, there's nothing more to be done at present and I can't stay. If you find anything then let me know first; we'll decide together what's to be done.'

The next day Behr and his successor entered the Director's office. The younger man, as senior restoration specialist, made the formal report. Artificial siccative had indeed been found on the backboards of the painting, and there were traces of chrome alum in the plaster. There could now be no doubt that the recovered item was not the original Leonardo, but a very skilful forgery.

What was to be done?

They at last decided that their only option was strict secrecy. If the thieves thought their forgery had remained undetected, there was some hope that they might make some careless mistake. They might, given their apparent success, risk selling it at a private auction in London or Paris, but as soon as they heard that their scheme had been uncovered they would surely ship it to America and sell it on the black market. Then all trace would be lost.

They agreed on this course of action and the Home Secretary concurred. A few foreign police departments had to be informed, of course, so telephone calls were made to London, Paris, Berlin, Munich, Rome and Florence, while the Hungarian police made discreet attempts to find out how the forgery had been made. They searched not only in the capital, but in Sopron, Szeged, Miskolc and other cities throughout Hungary.

Their inquiries soon produced results. A photographic reproduction—the necessary template for any successful forgery—had been produced at the Hélios Art Institute in Miskolc. This was not done in secret, but as an open and straightforward commercial transaction. A customer had come in with the painting three weeks earlier, asking for it to be photographed and transferred to a life-size white board which he had brought with him. Nobody suspected the least foul play, since of course the theft remained a secret from the public. The work was recorded in the register, along with the price: one hundred and fifty pengő. The customer's name was listed as 'János Kis', but a name as bland and ubiquitous as this was in all probability a pseudonym. Still, whoever this János Kis was, he had used the same name to book his accommodation: he was listed at the Miskolc Grand Hotel as arriving that afternoon and travelling on again late the same evening. He was remembered by all the staff as a well-dressed gentleman of above-average height and great bulk, while the chambermaid added that he was 'a right cheery old card'. The waiter seemed to recall an old scar on his temple, but nobody else remembered it. Everyone, however, said that while his Hungarian was excellent, he had an unmistakable foreign inflection. He was clean-shaven, and balding on top. Where he had gone after Miskolc nobody knew.

Naturally, the police also tried to discover the identity of the forger, since whoever had produced such a masterpiece must be an artist of considerable skill. In Budapest there were only three real candidates and old Behr knew them all well, for they had learned their trade under his watchful eye. Of these three, however, he considered only one truly capable of such perfect work. He was an industrious old man and the only person Behr knew who had studied the early *cinquecento* techniques an artist such as Leonardo would have used. The method required a mix of tempera grounding with oil highlights, and took years to master. Whenever foreign buyers asked for a Renaissance reproduction, it was always to this elderly painter that Behr directed their inquiries; the other two were trained only in seventeenth- and eighteenth-century techniques. What was more, this particular Leonardo painting would have been especially difficult to reproduce: the hair, beard and clothing were indicated only with a feather-light touch of pencil or brush, and the forger needed great confidence and skill to follow these graceful lines. That he had succeeded was beyond doubt: were it not for the chemical analysis of the painting's back then nobody—not even Behr—would have been able to detect any discrepancies between the original and the reproduction.

These three suspects were questioned but all claimed to know nothing about it, and it turned out that the only one Behr considered a serious candidate—the old artist—had been in hospital for the past two months with rheumatoid arthritis. He was obviously innocent. For now, the investigation found itself at a dead end. The forgery still hung in the Italian wing of the Museum, and the whole affair remained a very closely guarded secret.

II

Extracts from the Diary of Tibor Vida

Palermo, 5th of March
What a fine place Sicily is! I don't believe there's another spot like it in all the world: rugged, snow-capped peaks, green plateaux, hillsides covered in vineyards and olive trees; even oranges by the coast! Up close, a grove of lemon trees can feel as lush and verdant as any equatorial jungle! And everywhere you go you're confronted by that sparkling sea, beneath a sky of cloudless blue...

I've already taken the new Lancia out for a spin. This is first-rate country to explore by motor car, with a fresh vista around every corner. What a stroke of luck that the fellow from the Austrian consulate was transferred and had to sell his car at short notice—right when I needed a new set of wheels! All I had to do was change the plates for Hungarian ones. She's an absolute beauty, and in a completely different class from any car I've owned before—the thing practically drives itself!

This, I should say, is only the fifth day since my arrival in Palermo, but I've done plenty of sightseeing already and it's a really splendid spot. I don't have much of a head for history but I know a thing of beauty when I see it, and I've never seen anything like this. There's Monreale, Cefalù, the Cappella Palatina… I've been slogging manfully through the museums, churches and palaces, and while there is no end of history to get to grips with, it's surprisingly pleasant to loiter in some pretty courtyard or other. Another thing I've noticed is that the tour guides here aren't quite so confoundedly importunate as in the rest of Italy: some are even capable of leaving you alone for five minutes if you want to take your time over something. Is it the Arab blood in this part of the country that gives them a mellower outlook on life? But then I've just read that the Spanish and the Greeks—even the Normans—ruled these parts for centuries too, so maybe they picked it up from them.

I'm staying at the Excelsior. It's a very fine hotel, and from my top-floor perch I can survey the whole city, right out to the bay, or towards the splendid bulk of Monte Pellegrino. I had a piano brought up to my room so I can work on my newest operetta, but the truth is I've barely touched it. It just isn't coming at the moment. The sting I got from you-know-who is still too fresh. A wound to the pride—or my masculine vanity at any rate. Not that I've always been a model of fidelity myself, of course, but it's my first taste of that particular medicine from the receiving end. I suppose that's why I came here: air out my skull a bit, as they say back home, and do some travelling alone. Solitude has been good for me, but today, and for the first time, I felt it weigh on me a little.

Nothing in excess, as they say...

There aren't many tourists in the hotel—we're out of the high season, after all—so I seem to be sharing the place with nobody except a few tubercular grandmothers and one or two young couples on honeymoon. There's nothing doing with the old consumptives, of course, and as for the young couples—why, they're even worse! All that cooing and billing, gazing lovingly into one another's eyes? Repulsive! That's why I left Taormina, when the Villa Timeo finally became intolerable. The whole place seemed to vibrate through the night to the rhythm of young couples embracing...

Good Lord, I must be getting old!

Still, there is one pretty woman in this hotel, and so far as I can see she's here alone. She arrived last night and ate dinner at the table directly facing mine. Once or twice she glanced at me with big, brown, languid eyes, and I think I detected some intelligence behind them. I wonder why she kept looking at me? But perhaps it was just chance.

In any case, when it comes down to it I'm not even sure I'm ready for another affair, after getting my fingers burned so recently. My confidence has been shaken, and when a man's age begins with a four it's probably time for him to give up that sort of thing. That's another reason I came here: enjoy Italy for a while, clear my head, then go home and find myself a nice little wife. Not some flighty, lissom little creature either, but a mature, dependable woman happy to settle down and become a housewife. '*Torschluß*', as the Germans say: shutting up shop. Or maybe I'll play the bachelor forever and live out my days in roving, unencumbered style. Without a woman. God, how I detest women! So what am I doing chasing after them at my age, with my temples turning grey?

I asked the lift boy what her name was. '*La Signora Anderson, di Chicago.*' An American. She's on the same floor as me, too. Why would she be travelling the world on her own? Maybe she's here to wait for someone; her husband, perhaps, or her lover. Or a friend, or a sister. Who knows? It's all the same to me, at any rate. She may do as she damn well pleases, so far as I'm concerned.

6th of March
I have made the acquaintance of Mrs Anderson. Quite by chance, as it happens; I certainly didn't intend it.

25

There is a large placard hanging in the lobby, with a text in French and Italian advertising an auction at which a certain Marquis Bentiruba will be selling off his family's art collection, including paintings, statues, embroideries, some furniture and a few bronzes. There must have been heaps of stuff to begin with; this one is advertised as the third and final sale. Anyone interested can view the objects for the next two days. After that the bidding begins.

I was just reading this, and thinking that I might drop by in the hopes of snapping up a bargain among the smaller pieces—a cigarette case, say, or an ashtray—when I noticed the brown-eyed woman standing next to me. She was reading the announcement too, and standing extremely close to me. Though her eyes were fixed on the placard, I could feel her observing me. Women are like that; they can fix their gaze somewhere else entirely yet observe you quite closely out of the corners of their eyes. What wiles they have!

I said hello at once, of course. What an ass I am! Her being, as I thought, from Chicago, I spoke English.

'Interesting, isn't it? Are you planning to view the collection?'

She turned those big, brown eyes on me and smiled.

'Certainly, I'd like to.' Then she went on in Hungarian, 'But why speak English? I'm Hungarian too, you know.'

She explained that she had lived virtually her entire life in Budapest. The surname came from marrying an American.

'And you live in Chicago?'

'No. Not any more. We separated and I moved back to Budapest. I still use the name though, and my old American calling card: it makes a tremendous impression on hotel porters.'

She gave an ironic little laugh. The laugh, I thought, of a woman who is used to keeping her real thoughts to herself.

We ate a late breakfast together. I told her my name, but nothing more—I wanted to keep my occupation a secret. No use, though, she knew it already. She knows that I'm a composer, and that my third operetta, *Shakuntala*, was an international hit, with two runs in London's West End. She also confessed that she had already recognised me by sight, having seen me down by the footlights at my latest première. That was why she had wanted to get to know me… She laughed again. It suits her very well, that laugh; a sort of low, rich sound like a turtle dove's billing.

Mustn't do anything stupid.

The above was written in a hurry; I'm off to see the Marquis's wares!

Eleven the same evening
Well, we went, and rather eventful it was too! There's an old palace in the centre of town, built in that late Norman Gothic style they call *stile chiaramontano* here. The intervening centuries have given it a bit of a battering, of course, but it's still an impressive old pile. Passing through

27

the entrance arch we entered a huge, empty courtyard and were met by a porter and two footmen. They were all fairly scruffy, unshaven types, but their frock coats were positive marvels of piping and gold braid. After asking for our visiting cards, one of them went up the steps. A moment later he was back, saying that '*Sua Eccellenza*' would receive us. Climbing the steps, we entered a spacious hall with big windows on either side. A skinny young priest was sitting by one of the windows, reading a little book that might have been a breviary.

'*Sua Eccellenza viene subito*,' he said—His Excellency will be here directly—then went back to his book.

The walls were lined with countless pictures and on both sides stood large, exquisitely carved stone fireplaces. There were also several free-standing suits of armour, as well as swords and various other business-like tools of medieval warfare mounted on wall brackets. A few bronzes and other smaller items stood on a table in the middle of the room. The ceremonial nature of our welcome, however, and the expectation that '*Sua Eccellenza*' might appear at any moment, meant we hardly dared so much as look around us.

Sure enough, before long the marble-framed door at the far end of the room opened, and the man himself appeared before us. He really did have the most strikingly aristocratic appearance, with a spade-shaped, russet beard and pomaded hair severely slicked back. He was also dressed in a remarkably elegant suit, with a camellia in his buttonhole and a silk handkerchief in his breast pocket. I remember noticing in particular his two-tone, patent leather shoes in black and fawn. He greeted us with surprising conviviality, as kings do when deigning to receive a commoner. He even shook hands with both of us—though perhaps with a touch of condescension—and sat us down in a pair of very beautiful and very uncomfortable chairs. (These were for sale as well; a price tag hung from each.)

We began talking. The Marquis spoke fluent French, though of course with an Italian accent. He asked how long we had been in Palermo, what we had seen, and whether we had visited much of the surrounding area. He seemed not to hear our replies, giving us barely a moment to speak before asking the next unrelated question. He spoke as though all Sicily were a personal possession of his, and graciously invited us to make ourselves at home. He offered me a cigarette, and from politeness I asked whether it was permitted to smoke it in the exhibition space.

'Permitted?' he snorted. 'How should it not be permitted, here in my own palace? Any guest of mine should not want for the slightest thing while here. That is the ancient tradition of this palace. Everything for the comfort and convenience of an honoured guest.'

The man's grandiloquent style was beginning to wear a little and it was a relief when a tousle-haired man burst through the door and hurried over to the Marquis. As soon as he reached us, a torrent of voluble Italian burst from him, as though a dam had broken. Our host raised a finger to silence him, then turned to us.

'Please, do excuse me for a moment. Feel free to look around until I return.'

He handed me a copy of the auction catalogue, then departed with the newcomer. He seemed to be soothing the man as they walked.

'Yes, very possibly. That should be all right…'

We began inspecting the items for sale. There was not, in truth, a great deal on offer, but one or two things caught my eye. Among the pictures I found a Guercino, two portraits listed as belonging to the school of Antonello da Messina, and a few Baroque landscapes. All were ludicrously expensive, of course, and in any case, I had no intention of buying paintings. My attention was drawn to the table of small, ornamental *objets d'art*. One snuffbox in particular was very fine: it was made of tortoiseshell, with a gold inlaid coat of arms in the middle. I was just looking it up in the catalogue when Mrs Anderson, who had gone a little further than me along the line of pictures, spoke to me over her shoulder.

'Do you have the catalogue? Could I see it for a second?'

She was standing in front of a picture. It was not especially large, and showed a young man's head against a light background. The frame was a very simple affair of cheap pine, and it had been hung much too low on the wall;

one had to stoop to get a good look at it. Mrs Anderson, who was doing just this, looked up.

'This is very odd,' she said distractedly. 'Peculiar…' She shook her head. 'What does it say about 579B?'

It took me a long time to find the entry, which was not listed with the others, but separately at the bottom of the last page.

'*Head of Christ*. Copy after Leonardo from the mid-eighteenth century,' I read aloud.

'How odd,' she said again. 'This is exactly the same as the Leonardo in the Budapest Fine Arts Museum. It came from the Esterházy collection, I think… But I mean *precisely* the same! What are they asking for it?'

I looked back at the catalogue.

'Just two hundred and fifty lire.'

'That's it? As cheap as that? How very strange…' She looked back at the painting, her brow furrowed.

At last, though, we had to move on. Night was beginning to fall, so we departed without waiting for Marquis Bentiruba's return.

As soon as we were out on the street, Mrs Anderson told me she had to go. What on earth for? I asked. It was a fine evening for a stroll. She agreed to accompany me for a while, but hardly spoke; her mind was clearly on other things. I have noticed, I should add, that she is not much of a talker at the best of times. Before we took a taxi home, she abruptly announced that she had to send an urgent telegram, so I walked her to the post office. Eager to help, I even offered to lend her my fountain pen, but she said she didn't need it. I asked whether I should wait for her and she said yes, if I liked, and hurried inside. What could be the trouble that came up all of a sudden like that? Had I offended her? What was the meaning of that little crease in the middle of her forehead? She emerged soon enough, though, and we took a taxi back to the Excelsior together.

By dinner she was cheerful again, so maybe she's just a capricious little thing. Or did something remind her of an unpleasant character from home? Someone she depends on, perhaps, or fears? Who knows? What the devil do I ever know when it comes to women? They always hold so much back. Even this one, with those big, expressive eyes… Anything at all could lurk behind them! Yes, Even this one, this Milla—that's her name—Milla. Camilla, probably. Or Ludmilla, perhaps? She just said Milla. 'Milla with two ls.' That's what she said.

It's a nice name.

Better keep my wits about me! She could be a con artist or a pickpocket for all I know. I don't think so, though. No, I'm certain it's nothing like that. Still, there are women a good deal more dangerous than pickpockets!

The wisest thing would be to travel on first thing tomorrow.

Then again, she is very sweet, and really quite strikingly attractive… If I were a few years younger…'

But no! No, no, no! I don't want to start anything of that sort! No!

When we said goodnight I kissed her hand. I always kiss women's hands when they're young; never when they're old. A well-groomed, elegant little hand, and she gave it willingly enough, even letting me hold it a trifle longer than usual…

7th of March

I took her out to Monreale for a jaunt in the Lancia. It was a very pleasant trip and I was surprised by her knowledge and passion for art. Sometimes, talking about some work or other, she gets so carried away she grabs my arm, her big eyes even wider than usual.

We got back around lunchtime and stayed in for the afternoon. I had tea brought to my room and played the piano for her. I even went back to a few things hardly anyone remembers these days, like Bálint Balassi's 'Song for the Cranes.'

'Lovely!' she said.

Who knows? Perhaps she even meant it.

When she went to dress for dinner I stayed on for a while at the piano. For the first time since I got here I felt the stirrings of song within me. I picked out the rudiments of a moonlight theme, and it's got a pleasant little swing to it.

Women and music, music and women; they're inseparable. Or they are for me, at any rate.

Same evening, around midnight
I'm going to end up doing something stupid again!

8th of March, evening
Too true! Dear God, what a country! You can't keep a poker face in a place like this. How could anyone, strolling beneath such a crystalline blue sky, sweet balsam on the breeze and a thousand flowers bursting into bloom all around, help expressing what one feels? Impossible!

I dare say I could keep my emotions in check on Spitsbergen or in Greenland, with another icy fog rolling in off the Atlantic and gales of driving sleet, but in a place like this?

In any case, I'm not so old as all that, and I've never been blessed with the wisdom of Solomon, more's the pity. More's the pity? But why should it be a pity? Hang it all, we only live once, don't we? And even wise old Solomon had his fling with the Queen of Sheba…

My word, but she's beautiful! So, so beautiful!

True, I still don't know the first thing about her, but who on earth cares? In a few days, or a week—ten days at most—I'll be travelling on. We'll part, 'she down one road, I another…' Where did I read that? I can't remember. We'll have a brief, passionate romance, then part. Those are always the best. 'One kiss, then goodnight; certainly, sweetheart, of course I'll write.'

And nobody ever writes.

Yes, that's the best way. It certainly won't go on longer than a week or two. How could it?

Still, she's something special all right; so special I've already rechristened her. I always rechristen the women I sleep with if I really feel something for them. It's as though with a new name they're really mine. Maybe there's something primal in it, something atavistic, as in those cultures where they believe that knowing the name of something gives you power over it. I think I have a similar notion. All the other men she's been with have known her as Milla, whispering it in bed… They've profaned the name. But then, between two bouts of lovemaking it struck me: Milolu! How could anyone murmur 'Milla' in a lover's ear? But the sweet glides, the open vowels of 'Milolu' are like a verbal caress, and I'm the first man ever to call her that; she's never been anyone else's little Milolu but mine…

What an ass I am!

9th of March
This morning I slipped a little something to the porter and asked him to check the register for her details. After all, a man has to know something about the woman he's sleeping with. He told me that according to her papers, her ex-husband is T. W. Anderson, and her maiden name is Mária Radák. She's a journalist with the newspaper *Az Est*. They must be covering her expenses: this is a pricey hotel. I doubt she'd be able to stay here otherwise, unless she's a wealthy

35

amateur journalist who only writes an article or two when the occasion arises.

The same evening
A waltz emerged from the piano this afternoon and I called it *Milolu*.

Milolu, Milolu, Milolu…

It runs up through about twenty ascending arpeggios, then drops in a rippling, laughing glissando before climbing again. The whole thing is set off by a low, chromatic accompaniment in the bass. Oboes, maybe? Cellos? We'll see. I'll have to write some lovestruck text for it when I get home.

She's been on edge all day, and particularly this evening. It started late this morning when the trains arrived, then the Naples ferry. She didn't want to go anywhere, not even for a stroll around town. I wonder who she's expecting? Obviously she is—or at least was—waiting for someone. Nobody came, though; I kept close but inconspicuous watch, which is a thing I have a particular knack for when the need arises. No visitor came upstairs and the hotel switchboard operator told me that nobody called her room. It would have been *extremely* vexatious if some former lover of hers had chosen this moment to stick his oar in. I only want a nice, brief little fling, of course, but for some young buck to stroll in now and take my place? It doesn't bear thinking about.

We ate dinner in silence, but the atmosphere was markedly less tense than before, as though she had taken some definite decision. Later we had a very pleasant, natural conversation, and the subject of tomorrow's auction came up. She had a copy of the catalogue and asked me if there was anything I intended to buy. She agreed that the snuffbox was very pretty but particularly recommended that I snap up that cheap *Head of Christ* reproduction, arguing that it was an absolute bargain. I said I'd be happy to buy it for her if it would make her happy but no, she doesn't accept gifts, apparently. 'Well,' I said, 'buy it yourself!' She just smiled and said she didn't have the money for an expensive hobby like art collecting, but that I should absolutely jump at it.

'You'll see,' she said. 'You won't regret it!'

She gave a sly, expressive sort of smile that a man could read a lot into.

Is that really sensible? There's something in her, something in her words, in her smile—really everything about her—that leaves me just a trifle uneasy. It's as though there's always some secret, something unspoken, always hiding behind those big eyes… Something quite at variance with the person she presents to the world. With a different—what? Some plan or scheme? Is she trying to lure me into something? What? Why? Dear God, the way she looks at me with those eyes! And I haven't the faintest notion what they're hiding.

Two in the morning
As she was leaving, she repeated what she had said at dinner. The auction begins at nine tomorrow morning, and

I absolutely must be there. Why? Why is she so determined to have me buy this painting when she won't accept it as a gift? Maybe she'll take it after all, and pretending otherwise is just a tedious little conceit of hers.

10ᵗʰ of March

Well, I bought the picture. It's hanging over my fireplace now, though what good it will do me I still fail to see. I can't even take it back to Budapest with me, since even there I live in hotels. I could hardly have done otherwise, though, the way Milolu continually pestered me about the blasted thing.

She came with me, and in fact by half past eight she was already knocking on my door.

'Come on, it's time we were off already! We'll be late!'

The tables which had stood in the centre of the Marquis's great hall now lined the walls, and the space was filled with a great many wooden chairs. Bidders, by contrast, were in noticeably short supply and the only ones who looked like major players were two German lawyers who had presumably been sent to bid on either the Guercino or the Antonellos. One was from Mannheim, while the other was actually Swiss, from a firm called Reinhart in Winterthur. I learned this because the Marquis proudly whispered their identities in my ear. He evidently considered these two the only guests worth honouring. They were seated apart from the rest of us and, to reinforce their good humour, were liberally plied with glasses of Cinzano Brut.

The remainder of the gathering was made up of a few local auction hawks and a group of English and American tourists. The latter were exclusively on the hunt for smaller items, and one of them got his hands on the little tortoiseshell snuffbox I'd had my eye on. By the time the bidding finished it cost two thousand lire, which of course was miles outside my price range.

All this happened later, though. The auction was opened by a rather short gentleman who stepped onto the raised dais at one side of the hall and read out what sounded like an official proclamation in Italian. The gist seemed to be that he declared the auction legal and above board, and guaranteed that the buyers would receive their purchases shortly after the sale was agreed. My attention, I must admit, was not fully engaged, because Milolu's nerves were palpable. I could have sworn she was trembling! I asked her what the matter was but she said it was nothing. Then the auctioneer lifted his hammer and the proceedings began.

The pictures were presented one by one, to general indifference. They were, in truth, a fairly insipid lot, my Christ head included, but when its turn came I obediently lifted my pencil. The auctioneer asked if there were any takers for two hundred and sixty, and two or three men nodded. After a bit of desultory bidding I won the thing for three hundred and eighty lire.

Milolu at once gripped by arm with surprising strength, then leaned in and whispered in my ear.

'Go up and get it! Hurry!'

I frowned. 'Hang on a minute, what about my tortoiseshell snuffbox?'

'Oh, forget the snuffbox! Get the painting now! There's no time to lose!'

What need she feels for such nervous urgency in everything to do with this rather flat religious painting is entirely beyond me. I must ask her about it sometime: I've rarely seen anyone quite so—driven. In any case, I went up to the podium and one of the auctioneer's assistants gave me a little tag. Then I was led through to a side room where I paid. By that time Milolu was back at my side. She said that we would take it straight away, and requested the written receipt we were legally entitled to, stating that we had bought it here at this auction.

While they were writing the official receipt and affixing the necessary seals, the Marquis strolled over to congratulate us, speaking with the same condescending courtesy as before.

'You got a good price for that little number. I believe if I had held this auction during the high season I might well have got a thousand or more for it. You'll want to take it home, I presume? Feel free: the '*Lex Pacca*' prohibits the export of artistic treasures but does not cover later reproductions of this sort.' He made a little gesture with both hands, almost as though in benediction.

We went back into the main hall, holding the painting between us.

The auction was still underway, but Milolu—entirely calm now—did not want to stay.

'Oh, it's sure to be awfully dull. The only interesting things left are the little ornaments and they won't come up for ages yet. Let's go for a walk outside instead; it's a lovely morning. In fact, if you want to stay I could just go back to the hotel on my own and wait for you on the terrace. And—well, I might as well take the picture with me.'

She made this last offer almost as an afterthought, but I sensed she had been planning it for some time.

'By yourself? That wooden frame is heavy.'

Drawing me close, she kissed me.

'Oh, that's all right, I'll just take a taxi.'

I walked her downstairs to the street and she set off alone.

I was just walking back up the stairs when a man came bounding past me; he was taking the stairs three at a time and going so fast he almost crashed into me. It was the same hairy, squat little man who had hurried in to see the Marquis during our first visit.

I climbed more slowly; these old Gothic palaces have steep, stone staircases and I didn't want to trip. At the top I ran into some sort of blazing row in the doorway of the side office. The hairy man and the Marquis were—and this is no exaggeration—shrieking at one another, the words pouring from each without so much as a pause for breath. I hadn't the slightest idea what they were saying, nor why they might be so incensed, but it was probably nothing so very important. These southern Italians can have a minor tiff, forgotten in an hour, which to us more northerly types seems the prelude to mortal combat. Nobody else, at any rate, seemed to pay it the least notice, so I suppose it's all part of normal life here.

Nor did it last long; soon the hairy man threw his arms in the air, exclaimed '*Corpo di Bacco!*' one last time, then charged off as energetically as he had arrived. They're certainly a dramatic bunch, these Sicilians!

I stayed until noon on account of the snuff box, but, as I say, nothing doing. Disappointed, I strolled back to the hotel, where I found Milolu waiting for me in my room. She was sitting in front of the glass balcony door, the picture in her lap, lost in contemplation. Noticing my arrival at last, she leant it carefully against the fireplace and came over to me with a broad smile.

'Thank you,' she said. 'Thank you so much for buying the painting. It's beautiful!'

'But look, if you really like it so much, why won't you accept it as a gift?'

She just shook her head.

'It isn't even much,' I pressed. 'Three hundred and eighty lire really isn't so outrageous for a gift. Back in Budapest a big bouquet of flowers or one of the better chocolate selections from Gerbeaud wouldn't cost much less. I'm sure you'd accept something like that from me, so why not this?'

She shook her head again, and for an instant I thought I saw something like scorn glint in her eyes. Her voice, though, remained warm and sweet.

'What an absolute dear you are! I can't tell you how grateful I am and how pleased that you bought something like this on account of me. I know it was because of me that you bought it, just because of me, and I think you deserve a reward...'

She pressed those soft, red lips against my own. What a marvellous kisser she is! Honey sweet, with just the right mix of innocence and artfulness... What can I say? Like some love-struck puppy, I immediately forgot everything else in the world.

I didn't even close the door!

The same day, around six in the evening

The Marquis paid me a visit earlier. His card was brought up first and I've still got it here in front of me. The man has God's own list of titles:

Il Marchese ERCOLE BENTIRUBA degli Principi Orsinelli
Gran Falconiere Ereditario di Sicilia
Gonfaloniere di Calabria
Siniscalco Perpetuo di Pantelleria
Domestico Supremo d'Acchaia
Ammiraglio delle Galere del Regno
Conte-Duca d'Avila, di Grottarotta, Sciacca,
Leonforte e altri castelli

Or, in rough translation:

The Marquis ERCOLE BENTIRUBA of the Princes Orsinelli
Hereditary Grand Falconer of Sicily
Gonfalonier of Calabria
Perpetual Seneschal of Pantelleria
Supreme Chamberlain of Achaia
Admiral of the King's Galleys
Count-Duke of Avila, Grottarotta, Sciacca,
Leonforte and other castles

Etc. etc. etc. He's also some sort of Spanish grandee and a 'Rich'Hombre d'Aragon.' Spiffing!

Judging it unwise to keep the Perpetual Seneschal of Pantelleria waiting, I had him sent up at once. We sat down and each lit a cigarette, then I asked him to what I owed the honour.

With cheerful, lordly off-handedness he said he had come about the picture.

'I shall speak frankly, sir, taking you for a gentleman of honour and feeling.'

His explained that his wife, the Marchioness, was extremely upset about the sale of the picture. It was not, he hastened to add, a matter of monetary value—in this case very negligible—but rather of sentiment. That painting had been in the family for many generations and his wife had not been aware that it was to be auctioned off. Now she was extremely upset with him, and had wept continually all afternoon.

Most disagreeable.

'You will naturally understand, sir, that I do my best to be a good husband, and to behave as a man should when he loves and honours his wife.'

That was why he had come: to ask if the picture might be returned. If I consented, he said, he would give me a picture of immeasurably greater beauty and value, having in his possession many such works. He would be happy to part with a thing of ten times greater value than this little reproduction if it restored his wife to happiness.

He spoke persuasively, with an open, straightforward gaze and a smile both friendly and a little bashful. Had it not been for the thought of Milolu I should have given it back at once. As it was, however, I felt obliged to refuse.

The Marquis then went on to list other circumstances, explaining the situation in rather more detail. The problem was, he said, that the picture was not in fact his at all, but his wife's, having formed a small part of her dowry. Until now it had always hung in the little chapel where she said her morning and evening prayers—I would surely see, he said, that this was no simple change of heart or passing caprice. Entirely without his wife's knowledge… The sale had, in point of fact, been quite out of order.

'Though of course the fault lies with me alone,' he added quickly.

But surely I was a man of sufficient sentiment and goodwill to restore the harmony of his home by complying with this one small request?

His regret seemed so plain and heartfelt that I felt more than a twinge of sympathy. (He was, as I soon discovered, a man of considerable acting ability, but, being still unaware of this, I was on the verge of caving in to his request.) Without Milolu's acquiescence, however, I felt unable to comply. I telephoned her room but it rang and rang with no answer. Then I called the hotel porter and asked whether she was downstairs in the hall. He said she had been, but had then gone out for a stroll in the neighbouring English Garden with 'an unknown gentleman'.

'A what? Who? From the hotel?'

'No, *signore*, he came from somewhere else. Nobody recognised him.'

Well, this was a shock. So far I had been under the impression she had no acquaintance in this town, and I don't mind saying that the idea of some other fellow taking her for a stroll in the park rather knocked me off balance. My first thought was to go after her and find out who he was, but first I had to free myself of my visitor. Wishing him to leave, I hardened my voice.

'I can't say yet, but I'll telephone when I've made a decision. We'll see…'

My tone was decidedly negative. Bentiruba evidently guessed that my decision depended on the woman I had

46

been trying to contact. He flashed me his most winning, most thoroughly Italian smile.

'*Anche qualche bella cosa per la vostra donna...*'—And some pretty thing for your lady too...

'No! No!'

I stood up, hoping to oblige him to do likewise. With a melancholy shrug he rose to his feet, and I accompanied him to the door. There he stopped, seeming to hesitate for a moment, then turned back; his expression was utterly changed and a new resolve glittered in his eyes.

'Sir, I must now tell you something I had hoped not to have to say. This business of the picture may create quite serious problems in my life. I confess to you that I have not so far been entirely frank, but I will now tell you the honest truth, and explain the extraordinarily difficult situation in which I find myself...'

Well, it transpires that our illustrious Marquis is nothing but a simple employee of the Palermo Art Company. They pay him on account of his grand aristocratic titles—themselves real enough—and because by hosting auctions in the palace, foreign visitors are convinced that they are not simply picking up an antique, but an ancient heirloom of the Sicilian nobility. He always pretended the goods for sale were part of his own collection but in fact the vast majority were 'items of miscellaneous origin'. These brought the largest profit, as the firm kept thirty percent of the sale price. The palace was in fact municipal property; he simply rented it, playing the lord of the manor, so to speak, as stipulated in his contract. This had so far been a successful strategy: rich English and American tourists seemed willing to pay significantly more if they thought they were buying straight from some aristocrat's private collection.

'The truth is, I've lived very comfortably on the proceeds…'

'But all those people, the footmen, the liveried servants; it must have cost you a fortune!'

'Oh, the Palermo Art Company handles all that.'

'Even the priest who met us when we came in?'

'Certainly! He is the guard, to make sure nobody steals anything. He looks much more picturesque in a priest's cassock, and doesn't stand out so much.'

In this way—though of course with a great many more words—he explained the actual nature of the business. Items to be sold at auction were assessed by an expert in antiquities, who assigned them a minimum price. The municipal government agreed not to interfere so long as the license costs were paid promptly and in full, but this arrangement depended on a scrupulous adherence to auction-house standards: they always had to ensure that while the prices were somewhat inflated, the goods for sale were genuine antiques as advertised. Nevertheless, when it came to the less valuable items, their standards sometimes slipped, as had unfortunately been the case with the Leonardo reproduction. It was brought in at the last minute, while the catalogue was being typed up, and though there had been no time for the expert to analyse it, the Marquis had decided to sell it with the rest. That, he admitted, was not entirely professional on his part, but he had not meant any harm by it.

'The truth is, I have done similar things in the past and it has turned out all right.'

The problem was that the man who gave it to them was outraged that they had sold it for such a low price. Though he himself had set the two-hundred-and-fifty-lira minimum, and said it absolutely must be sold, he was now menacing them with the most outrageous threats. He was, it transpired, the hairy little man I had seen on two occasions; he had been unhappy because he wanted it hung nearer the door.

'He said it should be by the door, where it would catch the eyes of visitors. Ludicrous! The better paintings are always at the far end. We indulged his little caprice, of course, but I cannot imagine it helped. In any case, he is now in a great fury, saying that if we do not return the painting he will tell the municipality we sold it without expert appraisal. It is blackmail, of course; he is a scoundrel of the worst sort! The trouble is that technically speaking his argument is correct, and if he reports me then I am sure to lose my license. The company will need a scapegoat, and as I authorised the sale, I am the obvious victim... This is my entire livelihood, sir; with the profits of these auctions I support a wife, a mother-in-law and five dear children. The youngest is only *so* big.'

Eyes wide, his two palms indicated a span which a good-sized rat would comfortably exceed. Then he placed a hand on my shoulder.

'Sir, I beseech you, help me! Surely a cheap eighteenth-century reproduction cannot mean so much to you that you are willing to ruin my entire livelihood!'

In that moment I really did feel sorry for this poor Marquis, eking out a living from his inherited store of titles. His eyes were glazed with a watery sheen, and continual efforts to wipe the sweat from his forehead with a handkerchief had left his normally elegant hair a disordered mess. This pleading, dishevelled aristocrat was a truly affecting sight, and I would certainly now have handed the painting over at once were it not for Milolu; it simply wouldn't be right to give it away behind her back. When I spoke, however, my tone was entirely changed; I now sounded friendly and encouraging.

'At this instant I'm not at liberty to give you the painting but I expect that we shall soon be able to honour your request.'

Bentiruba's face broke into a broad smile of delight, and he expressed his gratitude by grasping my hand and wringing it vigorously up and down for a considerable period of time. Again his manner seemed to change abruptly, and now there was something almost jubilant in his voice.

'*Son' a voi per la vita, signore, per la vita!*'—I am yours for life, sir, for life!

Now, at last, he departed. I waited until the sound of his footsteps had faded, then grabbed my hat and hurried after him, heading for the English Garden where I expected to find Mrs Anderson and this mysterious gentleman. I wanted to know what shadowy business she was conducting behind my back. I only got as far as the top of the stairs, though, when she stepped out of the lift looking cheerful and relaxed.

'Heading out?' she asked with a smile.

'I was going to look for you, actually.'

She must have heard the note of grim displeasure in my voice, because she looked back sharply.

'Ah, I see,' she said, then made a gesture as if to say, 'Not here. Inside.'

When we got back to my room and closed the door, I turned towards her angrily.

'So? Who were you with? Who's this mystery man of yours? You don't owe me any loyalty, I know that; you're not my wife. Still, I think I at least deserve to know. Doesn't that seem fair? It's so unexpected, and I'm not the sort…'

She placed a hand on my shoulder, looking at me with those strange, magical brown eyes.

'Silly boy! Don't worry; you haven't the slightest reason to be jealous.'

'What do you mean? Who the devil were you with, then? Some old friend?'

She just smiled.

'You'll find out soon enough, but I can't tell you yet: I'm preparing a little surprise for you. You'll see—it'll be quite something!'

'A surprise? Those aren't the kind of surprises I like!'

'Silly! You're my only lover,' she said in that deep, purring voice, then leant against my shoulder and kissed my mouth.

Well, what does a fellow do in such circumstances? He kisses, of course, putting all other business, as it were, to one side.

Afterwards I related my encounter with the Marquis. I tried to tell it as well as I could, including many affecting details: my sympathy for the poor man's predicament was entirely genuine. Milolu's eyes opened wide and I had the peculiar impression that some secret pleasure gleamed in their depths. She listened to the whole tale without once interrupting, but when I concluded by saying that we could hardly do otherwise than return the picture, she burst out laughing. Picking up a scrap of bread roll from the table, she tossed it at me.

'This is more than we need to give those crooks! Nobody is going to report the Marquis, even if they do threaten him. It's all talk, and in any case, his second story is probably as big a lie as the first.'

'I think he was telling the truth.'

'Well, that's also possible; they may have decided to threaten him. Still, nobody would report him, you can be sure of that.'

'How could you possibly know that? You're forgetting the Italian passion for vendettas.'

'Very well, I don't *know*, I just sense it. I've got an intuition that something funny's going on. Either the Marquis or whoever gave him the picture is playing a clever game, but so far it hasn't come off the way they hoped.'

'What do you mean?'

'Oh, Tibor, use your head! Two hundred and fifty lire is an absurdly low price even for a decent modern Leonardo reproduction, but for such an excellent, historic copy? Don't you see how ridiculous that is? It's also suspicious that they only brought it in at the last minute; they knew that under no circumstances could an expert be allowed to see it. Don't forget that according to the Marquis the seller wanted it displayed near the door; he was trying to keep it away from the good paintings. They didn't make all these stipulations so that more people would see it, but *fewer*! Low price, cheap frame and surrounded by bad paintings in a dim, forgotten corner...' Pausing for a moment, she frowned. 'I don't believe them when they say it's an eighteenth-century reproduction. Nobody in those days copied with such painstaking exactitude; the techniques hadn't been developed. An eighteenth-century work would look similar, but not *the same*.'

'You know the original that well?'

'Of course. It's one of my favourite works in the Budapest Fine Arts Museum. I can't count the number of times I've stood in front of it. Everything suggests, in other words, that some scheme is afoot and that this painting is worth a great deal more than you paid for it. Presenting it now, without any fanfare, right at the end of the season when almost all the tourists have gone home, hedging it all around with bad paintings... No, Tibor, something fishy is going on.'

'But—what would be the point?'

'You'll probably find this a bit far-fetched, but hear me out. Imagine you had come into possession of a valuable painting in a manner which was—how should I put it?— not exactly by the book. What would you do? How could you generate a sufficiently plausible paper trail to allow you to sell it in one of the great auction houses of London or Paris? What you might do is precisely what seems to have happened here. Find an auction ostensibly selling family heirlooms, which would credibly explain why it just appeared out of nowhere, then present it at the last minute so that no expert has time to examine it. You'd also need an accomplice, of course: one man sells, the other buys. Now you have a legitimately acquired painting, with a receipt from the auction house which would suffice for Seligmann's in Paris, or De Zwaan in Amsterdam, or even Christie's. Auction houses are always such sticklers for provenance.'

'You really think it's something valuable enough for someone to go to all that trouble?'

'Yes! If this is, as I suspect, a copy made by someone in Leonardo's own studio, it could be worth a fortune! Imagine the headlines this could generate: "*Newly discovered work from Leonardo's inner circle!*" The same thing Bredius did with Rembrandt's *Saul and David*.'

Milolu is utterly adorable when she gets going on the topic of art. Her explanation had a certain undeniable logic, of course, but mostly I just couldn't help smiling at the way she gets so fired up. I thought a doubt or two might keep her going.

'Very neat, but then why didn't they buy it? The only people who bet against me were those local vultures, and they gave up soon enough…'

'I don't know yet. Something must have interfered with their plans. Perhaps the second man was arrested, maybe even both of them; surely the seller would have done something if he'd been there in person.'

'Hm. You might have a point there, now that I think of it. The seller was that hairy little fellow who came in when we were speaking to the Marquis that first time we visited, you remember? And this morning, just after you left, he came charging past me as I was walking back up the stairs. Going at such a clip he almost knocked me down, in fact. When I got to the top he was already screaming blue murder at the Marquis in the office doorway.'

'Really? And you didn't tell me? But Tibor, this is getting interesting!' She smiled and bit her lower lip. 'Very interesting indeed!'

III

11th of March, noon

I'll write it down quickly, to get it on paper so it will stand forever in my diary, slapping me in my stupid face every time I open it. You oaf! You ass! You God-damned useless bloody fool of an ass! So you wanted to seduce women? You wanted to play Don Juan? You fool! You! Yes, you! Every blasted woman you meet can lead you by the nose, you spineless, insipid, useless worm! She baits the hook, and you waltz straight up and swallow it!

I can hardly write all this down, but I have to! I must!

I've got to see it for what it is; it should be tattooed on the back of my hand, or emblazoned on my bedroom wall in fiery letters. I've got to be faced with it again and again until I finally get the message through my thick old skull:

All women are deceitful snakes. Treacherous, thieving, lying, abominable snakes. Or at least they are with you, you puppy!

Dear God, I've got to pull myself together and put this down objectively, so the facts will stand as a stark, everlasting testament.

It was mid-morning, around ten or so, and I was still in my pyjamas and dressing gown. I've become a decidedly late riser on this trip. The bell rang, and a porter appeared with a visiting card. All it said was 'Schönberg-Belmonte' and in small letters underneath: 'Frankfurt Paris.'

I wanted to reply that I could not at present receive visitors but at that moment there came a single rap on the door and a big, broad-shouldered, heavily overweight man stepped into the room. His left arm was in a sling.

'Ah. What can I do for you?' I asked rather coldly. I'd been hoping to get some work done.

My visitor did not reply but simply smiled and extended an enormous hand towards me, then repeated the name on his own visiting card as though letting me in on a valuable secret. Then he strolled across the room towards the big armchair that stands in front of the corner mirror and sat down with a long, contented sigh. I remained on my feet, so he smiled and gestured at the armchair opposite. Inviting me to sit down in my own living room!

'*Prenez donc place, monsieur,*' he said, then immediately switched to German. 'But it's probably more agreeable for you to speak German than French, and in fact the same is true for me. I am originally German but I moved to Paris many years ago and became a French citizen.'

I sat down, but did not speak.

He began telling me what a splendid social scene Paris had developed since the Great War, becoming once again the centre of the civilised world. There were dozens of new theatres, each striving with the others to put on the most outlandish and avant-garde performances, and money was as plentiful as coal briquettes. He spoke cheerfully and for a long time, as though we were old friends reunited after many years.

As he was speaking, I observed this peculiar stranger. The back of his head was reflected in the mirror and I could see how a few long strands of reddish hair had been combed across his pate in perhaps the poorest effort at concealing baldness that I have ever seen; they were like staves across a sheet of music paper. On his left temple I could make out the faint puckering of an old scar, while his little eyes were almost lost amid fleshy cheeks. His mouth, by contrast, was very large, and though he perpetually smiled I had the feeling that this was rather from habit than any genuine pleasure.

'Anyway,' he said at last, 'let's get down to business!' He adjusted the sling with his right hand, then pointed at the picture hanging above the mantelpiece. 'I've come for that.'

'Have you indeed? And what exactly do you mean?'

'I had long planned to buy it, and the reason you got it was on account of this little accident'. He nodded at his arm. 'These confounded marble stairways, they're like ice! I was on my way to the auction when I slipped and broke my arm. One bone, at least; not the radius, the other one. Have you ever broken an arm, by any chance? Worst damned pain of my life! I even blacked out for a few minutes, and they had to take me to the hospital. I'm not staying in town, you see, but out at the Villa Igea, above the bay. Do you know it? It's the most expensive hotel in the area, of course, but a charming place…'

As he was speaking, or perhaps a little earlier, the door opened and *she* came in: that woman I idiotically christened

Milolu. She was wearing a hat, and in her hand she carried a parasol. Coming over to my armchair, she leaned on the back of it and bent down to the level of my ear.

'Who's this?' she whispered.

I passed her his visiting card.

'He's here about the picture,' I whispered back.

Schönberg-Belmonte pulled his great bulk into a slightly more upright position and went on,

'So as I was saying, I want to buy that from you. It's not the only thing on my list, but I want it. I'm an art dealer, you see, which I don't mind telling you is a damned lucrative trade, begging your pardon, madam. I decided to drop by to see if I couldn't persuade you to part with it for the right price. That's correct, I'm willing to pay good money for that little thing. I'm not, sir, the sort of man who counts the pennies! I make good money and I like to spend it generously!'

I looked at him coldly.

'I did not buy this painting for the purposes of financial speculation.'

'Come now, what's it to you? You're not a collector, you have no gallery, what good will it do you? You bought it because you saw it going cheap in an auction, but you've no real use for it. That's always the way with travellers in Italy: they buy every pretty thing they see, then don't know what on earth to do with it all afterwards.'

I couldn't help smiling at how accurately he guessed my feelings.

'I'll find a use for it,' I said. 'I might give it as a gift.'

He laughed.

'See? I knew it! Look, I'll tell you what. How about if I pay you a really serious sum of money for it? Say a thousand lire. With the auctions going as slowly as they are, I wouldn't be surprised if a thousand bought you something worth closer to fifteen hundred; perhaps a dress of fine silk...'

He glanced up at the woman standing behind me.

'Think of what you can get with a thousand lire! A fine bronze, perhaps, or a coffee service of Murano glass. The world is your oyster with a sum like that in your pocket! So what do you say? Do we have a deal?'

'I've already told you, it's not for sale.'

'But come now, why on earth not? Who feels so strongly about cheap reproductions? It's different for me, I can fob it off on some rich, tasteless American on the hunt for "classy Renaissance stuff"; that's all they're interested in. Tell me, though, why would a man of your discernment cling to a trifle like this?'

The two-faced liar behind me pressed her finger into my shoulder, and I thought she intended it as a signal not to hand over the painting. Accordingly, I rejected Schönberg-Belmonte's offer even more firmly than before.

He continued to talk, telling me that I should think carefully. Nobody was likely to make a better offer. He was only able to be so generous because he was a wealthy, well-connected art dealer who chanced to be in Sicily on other business, and because by reframing it and putting it in among his more valuable pieces he could inflate the price considerably. Steepling his fingers, he stared at the ceiling, then appeared to make a difficult decision.

'Very good, to hell with it! Three thousand! You cannot reasonably refuse that, can you? That's almost ten times what you paid at auction!'

The woman's fingers pressed into my shoulder again, and again I refused his offer.

'No? Really?'

His plump, cheery features now abruptly darkened and profound menace glinted momentarily in his eyes.

'I suspect, sir,' he said slowly, 'that in time you will come to regret your decision.'

Then, however, he broke into another jovial laugh. 'You know they call me Belmonte the fortune-teller, since my predictions so often come true. Or is it because I'm as fat as an old gypsy grandmother? Either way, I'll give you one last chance. Tell me what I would have to give you to have that painting.'

Then something entirely unexpected happened. Glancing at her reflection in the mirror, I saw the faithless jezebel standing behind me wink at my guest, her eyes gleaming seductively and with a coy smile on her lips! The expression couldn't have lasted more than a second or so, but it was precisely the same one I have seen on the faces of painted streetwalkers as they cock their heads and beckon with a crooked finger... It was all so sudden, so completely bewildering, that I could barely find the words to stammer a response.

'No—it's... No, I won't sell it.'

Then that scheming witch turned and walked from the room as silently as she had entered.

My guest continued to make small talk but it was obvious that this was only for form's sake. He made no new offers, and soon departed.

Astounded, I stood alone in the middle of the room. That woman! That duplicitous...! It struck me again how little I actually knew her. She had just winked at a portly, middle-aged stranger, even while her hand was on my shoulder! Practically offered herself to him! And what was that sly, wanton smile all about? What was going on? What kind of person was I dealing with? Yesterday she went out with some unknown man, and today this! Might she and Schönberg even be accomplices?

In this state of extreme agitation I charged along the corridor to her room, just three doors down from mine, but even before reaching it I knew I would not find her there. Sure enough, the door was locked. Might she be down in the lobby? But I could hardly go downstairs like this in my pyjamas! I ran back to my room, but it was just as it always is when one is in a rush: I couldn't find anything, and five minutes must have gone by before I was ready. Dressed at last, I burst from my room at top speed. Unwilling even to wait for the lift, I took the stairs at a racing gallop. They open on the first floor onto a wide, colonnaded cloister overlooking the hotel's central courtyard. At one of the marble-topped tables in that central courtyard, Schönberg was sitting with *her*. I made my way along until I was directly above them; I could hear everything! Every word! She was speaking.

'...but as I said, I'm sure I can arrange everything. It won't be cheap though, not cheap at all!' She gave a mocking laugh, and I swear no sound has ever cut me quite so deeply!

'Well, let us say five thousand lire to your friend, and ten thousand to you for your help.'

'What do you take me for? You think I don't know what's at stake? I'm not here to talk lire, I want fat American dollars.'

'What do you know?' Schönberg's voice again had a threatening edge.

She shrugged. 'Nothing definite, of course, but you're not quite such a skilful bluffer as you think, and your eagerness to acquire the painting suggests that it is very valuable indeed. How are you to get your hands on it? I'll tell you quite frankly now that it's impossible without my help. So tell me how much it's really worth to you, and be quick about it!'

She was in a hurry, I guessed, because she did not want me to find them together.

'All right, let's forget the lire and say two thousand crisp American dollars. Now how does that sound?'

She shook her head. 'Not enough.'

'Three thousand, then, but it's my final offer.'

'No. More.'

'More? You think you can blackmail me? I strongly advise against trying.'

Schönberg stood up, his great bulk undeniably intimidating. She too got to her feet, and for a moment they stood glaring at one another in silence. At last the man spoke, enunciating his words slowly and carefully.

'This is my absolutely final offer. I would, with grave misgivings, perhaps go as high as five thousand dollars. I want to be clear that I am making this offer because I like to solve matters of this sort amicably, but that I have other means of putting my affairs in order...'

She answered just as seriously, and with equal care.

'No. It still isn't enough. And don't think, sir, that I'm an easy woman to scare. I'll say it again: there is no way of acquiring that painting except through me.'

'We'll see about that!'

With that he clapped his fedora on his head and strode out of the hotel at a brisker clip than I would have believed possible for a man of his bulk.

She just stood in the middle of the courtyard looking at her upturned hands, moving the fingers as though weighing two potential courses of action or counting something. Then she glanced at her wristwatch and at once hurried out to the street, where a taxi happened to be passing. Hailing it, she jumped in and disappeared.

This has been—I am not remotely exaggerating—among the most utterly wretched days of my life. Wretched! Where did she go? After him? Has she changed her mind?

Or did she go to see the other one, the mysterious gentleman she spoke to yesterday?

Oh, who cares! I have to end this whole miserable business, and end it at once.

It's time to leave this place. Right now! I have to get away! Pack my bags!

But what about the picture? Take it with me? No, I don't want to see it any more. I've got to try something else!

My first thought was to wait until she got back, then toss it down at her feet from the third floor, so she could watch with her own greedy eyes as all her plans were smashed to pieces. Then I had a better idea. Suppose I do something that would hurt her even more? Some more exquisite torture? I'll tie it up in wrapping paper and send it to Schönberg for nothing! I'll even stick in a few lines so he knows that I sent it, and not her! I'll write now, to make sure he doesn't give her any money! Not a God-damned penny!

I'm looking forward to seeing her expression when she finds out that all her pretty plans have gone up in smoke! Then she'll have a taste of what I've gone through today!

The same day, seven in the evening
Events, once again, have turned out quite otherwise than expected. In fact, I ended up giving the painting to

Milolu—or entrusting it to her care at least—as a gesture of reconciliation. She still won't accept it as a gift.

As can probably be guessed, I now see things from an entirely different perspective: things were not at all as I had supposed.

But let's start from the beginning.

I was just getting down to that letter I was planning to write when a motor car pulled up outside the hotel. I don't suppose that on any other day I would even have noticed, but the events of the morning had set my nerves on edge. I hurried onto the balcony in time to see Milolu pay the taxi driver and walk towards the hotel.

Stashing the painting in the wardrobe, I slipped the half-finished letter between the pages of my notebook and paced around the room a few times, trying to pull myself together. I planned to appear aloof, icily unreadable.

She came in, cheerful and smiling, as though quietly proud of herself. The sight of my travelling valise in the middle of the room checked her.

'What's this? Are you going somewhere?'

'Yes. I am.'

Her expression at once changed, her voice becoming anxious.

'What's happened? You haven't had bad news from somewhere? Surely not family?'

'No, but I've made up my mind to go. Straight away, in fact; I've already arranged things with the garage.'

She looked at me in stupefaction.

'But—sweetheart, what's the matter? What's happened?'

She tried to come closer, to put her hand on my shoulder, but I stepped back.

'Please, I'll trouble you not to come any closer, and don't dare touch me!' At this my icy reserve collapsed and I snarled at her. 'Who the hell are you? What are you? What kind of scheming, heartless…'

I began, in a word, to curse her roundly, accusing her at length—and with considerable colour—of being a cheating, conniving harlot. I had seen her smile at that man in the mirror, I told her, and heard her plot with him in secret. And for what? What kind of perverse love of deception could motivate her to betray me when I would happily have given her the beastly thing for free! What was the point of all this skulking about, conspiring with ruthless bastards like Schönberg? And what about her mysterious little stroll the day before? Had she met Schönberg then too, and simply pretended not to know him this morning, or was this yet another character in some monstrous web of lies and deception, of whom I was still ignorant? It was literally sickening! Not merely outrageous but physically revolting! The thought of it made me nauseous! Was it all just for the fun of toying with me? Leading me like a ringed bull by the nose? Good God, what a fool I had been! To think I had almost fallen for her… But that was all over now! Over!

I screamed these last words.

'Over! It's over! I know the truth now!'

As I paced up and down, waving my arms wildly, Milolu sat down and watched me. Her expression was sympathetic, but there was also a hint of impish amusement at the corners of her lips.

'You poor thing. Oh, Tibor, I'm so sorry. You poor thing…' Despite the faint smile, her eyes gleamed with tears.

Far from finished, I continued to rave up and down the middle of the room for a long time, using more or less my entire store of curses and imprecations to damn forever the name of woman, but she simply sat in front of me with an unchanged expression of sympathetic commiseration, periodically clasping and unclasping her fingers.

'You poor thing, I'm so, so sorry…'

I began at long last to run out of steam. She never once defended herself or expressed any anger towards me, and so my own anger gradually evaporated. Her proximity had an effect too, as did her beauty. All that remained in the end was bitterness, and the painful memory of my disappointment. I almost felt like weeping. Part of me also began to feel shame at the truly vile names I had called her when my rage was at its peak. I sat down at the table and put my head in my hands, speaking through them in a quiet, resigned mumble.

'Just go. I'm leaving.'

She did not go anywhere, but stood up and came over to stand behind my chair, where she ran her fingers through my hair with almost motherly affection.

'You poor thing. I can't imagine how awful this morning's been for you. You haven't got the slightest thing to be upset about, though. I'll explain everything and you'll see exactly what I mean…'

She sat down opposite me and began.

First, she explained that ever since her return from America—around three years earlier—she had been working as a journalist with Budapest's biggest newspaper, *Az Est*, and specifically as a crime reporter for the past two years. Such work was not especially lucrative, but it did put her in a position to hear many things which could not be written about, and of which the public—either from 'political considerations' or because it would undermine police investigations—was kept ignorant. There were many interesting secrets, she said, but one of the most interesting was that the real Leonardo da Vinci painting had in fact been stolen from the Fine Arts Museum in Budapest. Though ostensibly recovered, the painting which now hung there was in fact a forgery, executed with consummate skill.

This, the police believed, could only have been pulled off by a highly organised group with international connections, so when she saw the painting here, her first thought had been to wonder whether it might in fact be the stolen original. That was why she had been so anxious to send a telegram that first night; she wired to Budapest, asking for a painting expert and a detective to be sent down at once. Only the detective had been sent, however, and he—the man she had strolled with in the park—had not arrived until yesterday. Worried that the painting might disappear forever after the auction, she at last decided to ask me to buy it, though as she was obliged to keep the theft a secret, and did not know for sure whether this was the original, she had at the time felt unable to tell me the whole story.

'That's why I was so nervous that morning, and so completely over the moon when you got it. I was imagining how tremendous it would be if you could be the man to return this painting to its rightful home. Imagine if I were the one who got to tell the story! Tibor Vida rescues one of Hungary's most priceless artistic treasures! Still, it was only a suspicion then; I had no way to be sure. The Marquis's visit made it all seem much more probable, but now I'm absolutely certain. Schönberg-Belmonte *needs* this picture. I was struck at once by that malicious glint in his eye, and I'm sure the plan was for him to buy it; he was only delayed by that serendipitous accident of his. If he was going to buy it, then I suspect that he was going to sell it, too, which means he might well be the leader of the group.'

'But that smile of yours… My God, it was awful!'

I buried my face in my hands once more, but Milolu just laughed.

'I learned that face years and years ago, when I was still at school. It was a secret game a few friends and I had; each of us learned a sort of private grimace, and made them so often that I can still do mine today. Look!'

She lifted one eyebrow and curled her mouth into an ugly, leering smile.

'Christ!' I exclaimed. 'It's awful! Stop it! Don't do that again, I don't want to see it!'

She laughed again, then smiled and shook her head.

'What strange creatures you men are! I think it was because of that expression that old Mr Anderson married me, and when he found out I wasn't like that at all he lost interest. That's a different story entirely, though; back to the point.'

Seeing that Schönberg continually raised his price, she decided to find out how high he would go. If he went high enough then she would know for sure that this was the original. That was what the two squeezes on my shoulder had been intended to signify, though I had failed to understand: she had wanted me to tease him a little, drawing him out with the prospect of a potential sale.

'Why didn't you just tell me so in Hungarian? He's hardly likely to understand that!'

'We don't know that for sure, and risking it in such a situation could be extremely dangerous. If he does catch our meaning then everything is ruined. The only thing that occurred to me was to bring him down into the courtyard and flirt with him, acting as if behind your back I might—you know. And it worked! He went up to five thousand dollars! Can you imagine? How much do you think he's hoping to get from this picture if he's willing to give *me* five thousand dollars for it? I'm sure now that it's the real, stolen Leonardo, so I took a cab down to where the detective is staying and set him on the trail. What I failed to do—and again, I'm so sorry—was to come up and tell you what I'd done. It's my fault; I had this notion of springing it on you as an exciting surprise, but I wanted everything ready first. I was so looking forward to it! That was stupid of me, and you have to believe me when I say I feel absolutely rotten about it. You're so sweet, and I put you through such a wretched morning...'

She came close to me again, breathing against my ear, and in a low, purring, kiss-imploring voice, murmured these words:

'You know I really, really do love you...'

And later she said this:

'From here on it should all be plain sailing.'

IV

She was wrong, of course, but in order to explain just how wrong, we are forced temporarily to abandon the diary of Tibor Vida and outline how the police investigation had been progressing in the interim.

That means going back a few days.

It was the sixth of March when Mrs Anderson sent the telegram, asking for an art expert and a detective to be sent to Palermo with the utmost urgency; on the next flight, if possible. It was imperative, she said, that the detective have enough Italian to liaise with the local police department.

An art expert, however, proved more than the bureaucratic machinery of the Budapest police department could cope with. A what? What number could you dial for a reputable art expert? A few queries meandered from department to department until the matter was at last allowed to drop.

Finding a detective who matched Milla Anderson's criteria proved almost as difficult, and some time passed before the right man was found. Hungary, after all, is hardly brimming over with fluent Italian speakers. At last, however, they alighted upon a certain Károly Lakatos, who as a young soldier in the Austro-Hungarian army had spent two years as a prisoner of war in Italy. His knowledge of the language, though far from perfect, would allow him to make himself understood. He had served on missions abroad too, though admittedly in Austria and Czechoslovakia rather than Italy. His father had been staff surgeon with a regiment stationed in the Bohemian town of Čáslav before the war, and when he was a child Károly had gone to school there, where he learned fluent Czech. Two months previously he had been sent to Czechoslovakia on a secret mission, with forged identity papers giving his name as Jan Novák. He performed his task there so successfully that upon returning to Hungary he was given an official commendation.

There was, then, a considerable delay between Milla Anderson's telegram and Károly Lakatos's flight south, and he only reached Palermo on the afternoon of the tenth, after the auction had taken place. It was fortunate, therefore, that her initiative and resourcefulness had already secured the painting. His instructions were to rendezvous with her as soon as possible and learn from her everything he could about the situation. Accordingly, he at once called on her at the Excelsior.

He would never have dreamed of taking a room there himself; rates in a luxury hotel of that sort were far in excess of his meagre 'operational stipend' and he could picture the expression on his superior's face if he tried to claim a stay at the Excelsior on expenses. Indeed, given that he did not have to return any unspent funds from his stipend, and having a large family to support, he generally tried to spend as little as possible, and to use any excess to supplement his salary. It was a source of great satisfaction to return home from an assignment abroad with a few hundred Czechoslovak koruna or Austrian schillings in his pocket. This abstemiousness had become a fixation of his, and he never spent more than was strictly necessary. As soon as he had time, he set about finding the cheapest possible lodgings in Palermo, and soon came across just the sort of thing he was looking for. In one of the narrow, ill-lit alleyways by the port stood a tavern by the name of 'Albergo del Paradiso', a name entirely at odds with the grim, insalubrious character of the place. If it could ever have been called a paradise, it was only so for the great herds of bedbugs which infested every mattress and blanket.

Such matters were of no concern to Lakatos, though, for as an unpretentious man and a devoted father, he was willing to do battle with such vermin every night if it meant he could bring home a little extra from his travels.

That was how the trouble started.

The tavern had—as these places generally do—an exceedingly bad reputation, especially since it was as filthy outside as in. It rose tall and narrow between two other buildings, with lumps of crumbling plaster hanging from its walls, while the slight misalignment of two grimy windows gave the whole edifice a vaguely cross-eyed look. It was generally frequented by people of 'ill-repute', and had received numerous warnings from the local police.

That was not the whole cause of the trouble, but it certainly did not help.

When Mrs Anderson stepped out of the Excelsior, intending to hail a cab from the rank on the nearby square, she found she did not have to: a taxi waiting on the far side of the street swung across and drew up beside her almost as soon as she had raised a hand. It had, in fact, been waiting there since morning, and if anyone else asked if he was free, the driver always shook his head.

Not to Mrs Anderson.

She was in too much of a hurry to get a good look at the driver, and even if she had it is doubtful whether she would have recognised him. In fact, she had seen him just five days earlier, for he was none other than the tousle-haired man who had interrupted her and Vida's talk with the Marquis Bentiruba, but he was now wearing dark blue sunglasses and had a hat pulled low over his ears in a manner suggestive of baldness. Mrs Anderson paid him when they arrived at the Albergo del Paradiso and immediately forgot about him, though instead of departing he remained by his car and rolled himself a cigarette.

The proprietor soon appeared, and Mrs Anderson asked for Károly Lakatos.

'The Hungarian who checked in yesterday? Yes, he's here, shall I fetch him for you?'

Even as he spoke a young boy hurried up the stairs.

'I've got to speak with you urgently,' she said, after greeting him. 'I have new and important information. Where can we talk?'

Any private conversation was plainly impossible in the narrow confines of the tavern, so they walked out along the adjacent waterfront and sat down outside one of the quayside cafés. She explained what had happened with Schönberg-Belmonte, describing him as a big, heavy-set man with an old scar on his temple.

'Now that's something!' said the detective. 'A member of staff at the Miskolc Grand Hotel described a similar man, a János Kis, as visiting the hotel; the same János Kis who made the photographic reproduction of the painting. One man remembered a scar exactly matching what you describe.'

Might they be one and the same?

It was agreed that Lakatos would head out to the Villa Igea and have a look round, to see if he could find out whether this man had any accomplices nearby. Returning, he would let her know by late afternoon or evening what he had discovered.

Mrs Anderson frowned. 'Couldn't we have him arrested straight away? I'm practically certain he's mixed up in the theft somehow.'

'I agree, but there hasn't been time to go to the police headquarters yet. Yesterday I had to hand over my passport to the tavern keeper, and this morning I'm afraid I overslept a little.' He thought back on that restless, sleepless night, but upon reflection decided that bedbugs were not a fit topic for such refined feminine company. 'I was tired from my trip,' he said instead.

'But you'll report him this afternoon?'

'Certainly! Just as soon as I've seen for myself where he stays and who he's with.'

'There's a bus route that takes you out that way,' she said. 'I don't know precisely where it departs from, but they'll be able to tell you back at your lodging.'

Then, knowing what was expected of a visitor at the Igea, and having noted Lakatos's conspicuous parsimony, she 'lent' him a hundred lire so he could dress well enough to blend in. Then, after some further conversation, she set off back to the Excelsior.

Returning to the Paradiso, Lakatos asked for a bus timetable and his passport.

'It isn't back from the police station yet,' the proprietor said. No mere stretch of the truth, this was a downright, barefaced lie, but we shall soon understand his reasons.

A little earlier, while Lakatos and Mrs Anderson were walking down towards the port, the taxi driver had approached him.

'Who's that man who just walked out of here?'

His voice was so urgent, so serious, that the proprietor took fright. His *albergo* was, if not quite a den of thieves and vagabonds, at least a haunt of the thoroughly disreputable, and had already been issued a 'last warning' from the police, but he nevertheless attempted to protect his guest with a few airy generalities about the foreigner's quietness and good manners. The hairy man—hardly a flattering appellation, but in the absence of a name it will have to do—interrupted him.

'I'm with the fascists!' he hissed. 'Better watch what you say!'

Lifting his collar, he flashed a silver lapel pin showing an axe-head wrapped in a bundle of rods; it was the *fasces*, the symbol from which the movement took its name. These little badges were ubiquitous in Italy at the time, though not official party insignia. The hairy man was not, in fact, a member of the fascist party at all, but he well understood how hated and feared they were in Sicily.

The terrified proprietor's resistance collapsed at once.

'*Prego, signore*, whatever you want to know...'

'Where's his passport? Has it already been submitted?'

'Not yet. He checked in very late last night and I haven't had time to deliver it yet...'

Hurriedly rummaging in the drawer, he found the passport and handed it over. The hairy man flicked through it, soon finding the largish piece of paper stuck inside. It was his official identity document from the Budapest commissariat of police. He took it out and read it, then stuffed both the document and the passport into his pocket.

'Highly irregular!' he said. 'Give me the key to his room, I want to see what he's got stashed away up there!'

Taking it, he hurried upstairs.

It did not take him long, since he was skilled in the art of swiftly rifling through another man's possessions. In the bottom desk drawer he found Lakatos's attaché case, and in it the high-quality forgery of a Czechoslovak passport in the name of Jan Novák. He thought for a moment, then went over to the bed and lifted the mattress. Shoals of bedbugs scattered in sudden alarm, but were soon able to resume their midday slumbers; as soon as the Czechoslovak passport had been safely stowed between the bed slats and the mattress they were enveloped once more in restful darkness. The hairy man went back downstairs.

'What's this scoundrel's name again? Lakatos? And he's really a Hungarian?' He went on without waiting for a reply. 'Here's your key. It's my guess there'll be an official police search soon, but if you breathe one word to him of what's coming then we'll shut this rat-infested doss-house for good!'

'*Per favore, signore*, I've done everything you asked. I won't say a word, I swear!'

The hairy man departed and the proprietor breathed a sigh of relief, but his heart still hammered. After all, the precarious nature of his establishment made the man's dire threats all too plausible.

The hairy man returned to the Albergo del Paradiso a little after Lakatos had set off towards the Villa Igea, bringing with him a bulky package with squared-off edges. It was neatly wrapped in paper, as official documents generally are when sent by post. He took the key again and set off upstairs, returning again after just a couple of minutes.

Another half hour passed, then a squad of policemen arrived alongside a black-shirted commissioner. The hairy man was also present, but only as an informant.

They all went upstairs and the room was thoroughly searched. They soon found the passport hidden under the bed, of course, but also something much more serious: anti-fascist propaganda printed by Italian émigrés in Britain and smuggled back into Italy, most likely from Malta.

An official report was written up and they confiscated the Hungarian passport, which the hairy man had returned to the proprietor after his last visit—though of course without the official identity papers from the Budapest police.

Police officers were stationed nearby in preparation for Lakatos's return, and as the proprietor had informed them of his guest's inquiries as to the best way of reaching the Villa Igea, suggesting that this was where he had gone, a telephone call was made from police headquarters to the *carabinieri* station at Acquasanta, just down the road from the villa. They soon established that the signature on both passports was identical, but assumed that the Hungarian one was the forgery and the Czech passport genuine, otherwise why would he have hidden it? The *carabinieri* were therefore instructed to arrest a certain Giovanni Novák, who also went by the Hungarian alias of Carlo Lakatos, and who sometimes pretended to be a secret agent for foreign governments. The investigation was soon recorded as the 'Jan (Giovanni) Novák state security case' and stamped with the word '*segretissimo*'—top secret!

Poor Lakatos had not the faintest inkling of these developments. He got off the bus a stop or two before his destination and, seeing a cheerful, informal little restaurant of the sort Italians call an *osteria*, went in and ordered a large risotto. Not for him the affected manners and extortionate prices of a hotel restaurant! (This distaste for fine dining would come to light later, and was considered further grounds for suspicion.) Still, afterwards he decided to indulge in a post-prandial black coffee at the Villa Igea.

Entering, he found himself in a splendid hall full of elegantly dressed guests. Finding an empty table, he sat down and looked around. At the other end of the room, by one of the windows, he saw a man strikingly similar to Mrs Anderson's description of Schönberg, with his arm in a sling.

After scrutinising him at length, he summoned one of the waiters. This was important, he told himself; he would have to act with circumspection.

'Pardon me, there's a fellow over there by the window— yes, the big chap with the broken arm—who I'm almost sure is an old acquaintance of mine. You couldn't tell me his name, could you?'

'I don't know, *signore*, but I will find out at once.' The waiter hurried off obligingly, but he soon returned looking crestfallen. 'My colleagues do not know either, I am afraid. I could inquire further, if you feel it is important enough…' He cast a significant glance at the wallet lying before Lakatos on the table, but the detective only tipped him a few lire out of politeness. Knowing he would get nothing useful from the waiter, he sent him away.

He needed a new plan, and quickly: time was pressing. After paying for his coffee he got up and began to saunter idly between the tables, sitting down at last at the same table as his suspect. Without exactly looking at him, he scrutinised the older man closely. The resemblance was perfect, and he even managed to make out the faded scar on his temple.

Schönberg-Belmonte—for it was indeed he—pretended not to notice the newcomer's arrival, though he knew it could be none other than the Hungarian detective his accomplice had so recently warned him of. Schönberg's sunken eyes gave nothing away, and his eyelids were so low he seemed about to fall asleep. They remained like this for some time, until at length the other guests began to leave the dining hall. Lakatos decided he had to risk speaking.

'Fine view from here, isn't it? I don't believe there's another like it in all the world...'

He said this in reasonably good Italian, though with a strong accent. The old man seemed, however, either not to hear him or not to understand. He glanced briefly at his fingers, then gave a great yawn and rose lugubriously to his feet, setting off slowly towards the main stairs.

'Bastard!' Lakatos said under his breath. 'You heard me just fine!'

For want of any better ideas he approached the gold-braided concierge, slipped him a ten-lira note and asked to see the guest register, saying that a few of his friends were in town and he thought they might be staying at this hotel. Lakatos did not, however, mention any names, and the concierge allowed his experienced eye to linger for a moment on this slightly nervous young man with the peculiar smell. It did not take him long to convince himself that, whoever he was, he had some other motive besides a courtesy call. In any case, his furtive enquiries were in themselves suspicious, and having—as most hotel concierges do—contacts within the police, he decided to inform them of this stranger. The insultingly meagre tip also played a part, but he decided that for now he would voice only the vaguest of suspicions.

After glancing at the guest list, Lakatos affected a melancholy sigh. 'No, not one of them, I'm afraid. It was worth a try, at any rate…' He went to leave, then turned back. 'By the way, I couldn't help noticing a certain Signore Schönberg-Belmonte on the second floor. I don't know the man personally, unfortunately, but I've heard many good things about him. I was wondering if you'd noticed any of his friends around here? I know quite a few people in town, you see, and if we had a mutual friend or two who could introduce me…'

'It grieves me, sir, that I am unable to be of assistance in this matter. There are indeed two gentlemen who visit Mr Schönberg-Belmonte habitually, but neither stays at the hotel and so I do not know their names.'

'They're foreigners too?'

'I'm afraid I have not the slightest idea. One, I am inclined to suspect, is indeed Italian, but when it comes to the other I could not even hazard a guess.'

'And what happened to his arm? Was it some sort of accident?'

The concierge felt on safer ground here—the accident was hardly a secret, after all—so allowed himself to answer more freely.

'That was a very unpleasant affair, sir; he slipped right here on the stairs. You can't imagine what a thing it was to

84

see! The forearm simply shattered, as though it had been blasted from a *cannone*! Absolutely atrocious; he even passed out for a few minutes! Luckily there is a doctor living nearby, whom we summoned at once. I was the one who had to sprint up the hill to fetch him. Me! Then we sent someone into town to fetch plaster of Paris.'

He went on in this vein for some time, becoming gradually more impassioned as he described the deathly pallor of '*il Signore Belmonte*' and the fearsome curses he had roared in German. Beginning to enjoy himself, he tried to imitate the effect of these imprecations, lowering his voice and growling '*Crussi Turca... Donna Vetta... Ergotta Sacramento!*' and various other half-grasped utterances.

Reaching the end of this performance, it occurred to the concierge that he had offered rather more information than a miserable ten-lira tip deserved, and so he abruptly turned to examine the papers stacked on his desk.

Lakatos, by contrast, considered this a very small return on his substantial ten-lira investment, so continued to press for more information. When did he arrive? Did he have an expensive room? How much was he paying? Was he as rich as they said? The concierge's responses, however, were limited to a few non-committal shrugs.

'God, these Italians!' thought Lakatos, turning away. He had virtually nothing to show for his efforts. Were there any other options? Perhaps the lift boy, or the maid on the second floor? Yes! That was his likeliest bet. True, it meant spending even more money, but there was nothing else for it…

At that moment a serious-looking man in a dark civilian suit appeared in the hotel foyer. He walked straight over to the concierge, and the two men had a brief, whispered conversation, then the newcomer approached Lakatos.

'Pardon me, sir, I wonder if I could speak to you for a moment.' He spoke very politely, but there was a hint of quiet menace to his next words. 'I'm with the police.'

Poor Lakatos, failing to read the man's grave expression, was delighted; he assumed his official papers from the Budapest police department had made such an impression that someone had been sent to liaise with him in person. He smiled broadly.

'It would be my pleasure to be able to…'

The other man interrupted him sternly. 'Jan Novák?'

That was odd. How did they know about his Czechoslovak alias? Frowning, he paused for a moment before replying.

'No, I—Lakatos is the name. Károly Lakatos. I'm Hungarian.'

'We know about that one too,' the man said with a snort, then nodded to two tall, broad-shouldered *carabinieri*, who positioned themselves either side of Lakatos. 'You're coming with us.'

'I—I told you, I'm more than happy to,' replied the flustered detective, less and less sure of what was going on.

The situation would have appeared no clearer had he chanced to notice the overweight old gentleman with his arm in a sling who stood on the upstairs landing to watch, and who could not resist a quiet chuckle as Lakatos was led away.

At the corner of the hotel stood a car with tinted windows, and the Hungarian detective was invited to get in. The two *carabinieri* then got in and sat opposite him, service revolvers in their laps.

'What's going on here? Why...? There's been some kind of mistake!' said Lakatos, panic rising in his throat.

'*Silenzio!*' was the only reply.

Mrs Anderson spent the whole afternoon in the Excelsior, not wishing to miss any telegrams which might arrive from Lakatos. By seven in the evening she was becoming increasingly worried and decided to call the Albergo del Paradiso to ask whether he had returned yet. The reply, however, was terse in the extreme.

'*E partito.*'—He's gone.

The person on the other end of the line hung up immediately. She called back, but the same voice now said: 'Wrong number.'

What was going on? She called again a little after ten, but the reply was the same as the first time.

'*Partito.*'

How very peculiar! Had Lakatos really travelled on so quickly, without so much as telling her of his departure?

The only explanation she could think of was that Schönberg, getting wind of him, had made a break for it, with Lakatos in hot pursuit. This thought comforted her a little, though she remained irritated by the stubborn terseness of the *albergo*'s proprietor.

Had she understood the situation she would have been deeply grateful to the man, who had more wit than most people gave him credit for. He knew that the police would want to interview anyone in contact with Lakatos, and when Mrs Anderson first phoned him the police still had a guard outside. Hearing the first phone call, a policeman had come in to sit next to him, and that was why he had said 'Wrong number' the second time. Though terrified of the police, the proprietor of the *albergo* always sided with their fugitives and outlaw quarry, whether smugglers, political dissidents, stowaways or thieves, and it did not hurt that they generally paid well. It is very probable that, had he acted with less circumspection, both Milla Anderson and Tibor Vida would have joined Károly Lakatos in prison.

As it was they remained free for the time being, though from this point on their situation became considerably more precarious.

V

From the Diary of Tibor Vida

12th of March, noon

Something strange happened to me last night. Very strange indeed. I'm almost certain that while I was asleep I was knocked out with some sort of drug—chloroform, probably—and even as I write these words I still feel rather woozy from the effects.

What's certain is that someone else was in my room last night.

Nothing's missing; I still have my watch, my wallet, my documents, and everything else, but somebody has definitely rummaged through my clothes and underwear. Not that it's very conspicuous, mind you, but I like to stack my things in a particular order and now they're all mixed up. Whoever it was looked under the piano lid too; it had been closed again, but not locked, and I always lock it.

How did they get in? The door to the corridor was locked, with the key in the lock, and there's no other entrance. The only possibility is the balcony. There's simply no other way.

But how the devil would anyone get in through my balcony? Every room has its own balcony, and while they're pretty broad, they certainly don't meet one another. I'd estimate a gap of at least a metre and a half between my balcony and the next one, above a three-storey drop.

My neighbour to the right is an old Scottish lady who was already here when I arrived and who always says 'Very warm for the season' when we pass one another in the corridor. I can hardly picture her leaping between the guard rails of our balconies and gassing me. My neighbour to the left is a young man who arrived yesterday evening. He's a tall, broad-shouldered fellow who might be some sort of sportsman. I got a good look at him yesterday morning because he chanced to come into my room while I was shaving—or was it chance? He was very apologetic about it, saying he'd got the room numbers mixed up. He spoke English. His pronunciation was poor, but he definitely spoke English. Then he asked me something—was it about prices, or the restaurant or something? I can't say for sure, I'm still a bit light-headed. I remember him glancing round the room as he talked about whatever it was, then he apologised again and left.

Sometime after ten last night I put on my dressing gown and went over to see Milolu, then came back here at around midnight and went straight to bed. When I finally woke up I found it was already after eleven! The balcony door was definitely locked, both when I went out and when I got back, and the curtains were closed. Now both are wide open! That was what first caught my eye when I woke up; that and the hint of chloroform that I still get a faint whiff of every few minutes.

I'd better have a look around!

I didn't find anything concrete, but one thing adds to my suspicions. The glass door to the balcony is made up of a dozen or so panels, and in the lowermost one, right by the foot of my bed, a little hole has been punched through the glass, with a few fissured cracks spreading from it. It would barely be wide enough to slip a good-sized pencil through, but it's there, while everything else in the room has the look of being brand new and in immaculate condition.

I've definitely never seen it before. I don't remember inspecting the door very closely, and I suppose it's possible I simply missed it, but I don't think so. Especially since the hole meets the wooden frame at the top, and the wood there looks very fresh, as though it hasn't been exposed to the air for long.

Not being, by temperament, a believer in miracles, I've been attempting to explain to myself what might have happened. Say someone—perhaps my neighbour to the left, perhaps someone else—waited until I went up to see Milolu? He might well know about our relationship, since after all we've hardly been secretive about it and were together all day yesterday. He would probably have a fair idea of how long I'd be away, and in any case his business there wouldn't take much time. So, let's say he manages to leap across the gap to my balcony while I'm gone, then either bores that little hole with a diamond cutter or punches it with a spike. All he has to do then is wait until I've come back to my room and he's reasonably sure I've fallen asleep. Then he can slip a rubber hose through the hole—as I say, it's right by the bed—and pump in enough chloroform to knock me out. Then he must have picked the lock—it's a flimsy-looking thing—and opened the door. Did he open the balcony door and wait until the chloroform had dispersed a little before beginning his search? Or perhaps he had a gas mask, and only left the door open when he left so that the gas would disperse and I might wake none the wiser, thinking I'd left it open by mistake.

But why?

There's only one possible explanation: he wanted to steal the picture. What a stroke of luck that I gave it to Milolu for safe-keeping. The thing would have been gone without a trace if I'd kept it here! But what should I do now? Report it to the police? Or perhaps to the managing director of the hotel?

I'd better talk to Milolu first, but I'm told she went out a little while ago. The strangest thing is that this happened after—so far as we can guess—Schönberg-Belmonte scarpered! Who else knows about the picture? And who else would want it enough to risk breaking into my room?

I can't make head or tail of it!

Milolu came back with grim and unexpected news. It seems Schönberg-Belmonte hasn't gone anywhere but is still at the Villa Igea! That's where Milolu went this morning, to see if she might overhear something that would help us understand what happened yesterday.

She was just chatting to the concierge, asking him about room prices and the like, when she spotted old Schönberg sitting at the bar next door. He was sitting with his back to her, but of course a man that size with a sling around his neck is recognisable from just about any angle you please. Beside him was my next-door neighbour, who I had happened to point out to her yesterday evening at dinner. This fellow was facing her, so she got a good enough look to know for sure that it was him. He was in the middle of explaining something to Schönberg, and from the brief instant she watched him she got the impression that he was defending or justifying himself in some way.

She could not risk being spotted—and is confident she wasn't; they seemed very preoccupied by their conversation—so she quickly left and took the bus back here.

Afternoon, four o'clock

We had lunch sent up to Milolu's room. Neither of us wanted to go downstairs. I—still in my dressing gown—would have had to dress, and we were both too skittish and on edge to be seen in public. In any case, an urgent decision was necessary. What were we to do? It was hardly something we could discuss over French onion soup in the dining room!

Our situation appears grim, and there can be little doubt that Lakatos has fallen into a snare of some kind. Why else would he have simply vanished like that? I suppose they might have gassed him and taken him away somewhere, but a likelier and more straightforward explanation is that they've simply bumped the poor man off and tipped him over the end of the pier.

Anything could happen down by the harbour, in that seedy part of town he was staying in.

What this also means, though, is that they will stop at nothing to get the painting back, and that we're dealing with a thoroughly ruthless gang of criminals. If they didn't find it in my room, they're sure to try Milolu's next.

That means she's now in even greater danger than I am! Milolu!

I'd dearly like to go to the police, but what could we tell them? Schönberg trying to buy the painting from us is hardly a crime, and all the evidence that he's involved in the theft is gone with Lakatos and his official letter from the Budapest police. We could contact Budapest ourselves, of course, but it will be an age before they send someone else. Anything could happen by then! I've also got no way of proving that my room was searched during the night: nothing was stolen, and the only evidence is the little hole in the pane of glass. On its own that counts for nothing. Then there's the hotel management, who would be anxious to avoid any hint of scandal; they could even say the glass had been broken before my arrival, and with all his money Schönberg could easily bribe some maid to testify that she broke it a few weeks ago.

No, no hope there I'm afraid!

The only thing we can go to the police about is Lakatos's disappearance. We can say we know him, and that Milolu met him down by the harbour. All we know is that he went to the Villa Igea and disappeared, but the police should have his passport at least, so they can hardly pretend he doesn't exist.

Yes, that's the thing to do. If we both go to the commissariat of police together then they might take our report more seriously, and my command of the Italian language is, if I'm any judge, slightly superior to Milolu's.

First, though, there's the matter of the painting itself. We know for a fact that it's no longer safe either in my room or hers. The best thing would probably be to store it in the hotel safe, but we can hardly just hand the thing over as it is. It'll have to be wrapped in cotton padding and lots of paper, to make sure it doesn't get bumped or scraped. Besides, we don't want anyone to know what it is; that could be very dangerous indeed. Schönberg might learn of its whereabouts, and then who knows what might happen… I don't trust anyone any more!

Milolu says she'll wrap it while I change.

Afternoon, five o'clock
I had just finished scribbling the above and had got myself dressed when the telephone rang. It was Milolu, telling me to come up at once.

She sounded worried.

I hurried down the corridor, entering the room to find a strange, fat little man sitting next to her. He had olive skin and huge eyes the shape of plums, and apparently goes by the name of 'Pancia', which in Italian means 'belly.' I dare say it suits him. In any case, it turns out he's the proprietor of the Albergo del Paradiso, the little place down by the docks where Lakatos was staying.

This Mr Belly has a habit of wiping his forehead with a handkerchief and looking around nervously; when I opened the door he gave such a start he almost fell off his chair. He only calmed down at last when Milolu explained that I was a friend of hers. Still, he insisted that I close the door before continuing his story. It was a dramatic tale, and certainly lost none of its drama in the telling; he spoke quietly but with wide, sweeping gestures and bug-eyed expressions, like a messenger recounting the hero's death in a stage tragedy. I doubt Mozart could have found a better Leporello for the première of *Don Giovanni* than our Mr Belly.

In any case, he had come to tell us that we were in grave danger and should get out of this place at once. Not next week, not tomorrow, but now! Every moment was precious. We didn't understand, of course, and I asked him what he meant. Why should we run away? From whom?

'Sir, I'm sorry sir, but you do not understand what dangers are threatening you here!'

He was, he said, a friend to anyone hunted by the police, and would do the same for anyone in our situation.

'Believe me please, I'm telling the truth!' he said, putting his plump left hand over his heart and raising the other as though pledging an oath.

Despite the theatrics there really was something very convincing in his demeanour, and we've gone through too many peculiar things to laugh at a story just because it sounds unlikely. That was when he confirmed that Lakatos had been taken. Yesterday the police searched his room and found some kind of documents—anti-fascist literature, he thought—which led to his arrest.

'But that's impossible!' I exclaimed.

'Oh, sir, you are a gentleman, you do not know the way of these people; they planted it there themselves. That is what they usually do if they want someone arrested. One man plants, the other finds, and I know that is what happened this time.'

'Unbelievable! But who? Who did it?'

Pancia now leant forward in his chair, eyes almost starting out of his head, and spoke one word in a hoarse voice barely louder than a whisper:

'*Fascisti!*'

Indescribable hatred sounded in that brief utterance.

'Fascists? But why? What possible reason…'

'*Chi lo sa?*'—Who knows?

The little tavern-keeper went on to say that a guard had been placed around his establishment; they planned to arrest anyone inquiring after Lakatos. He had come here because *Madama* visited his *albergo* yesterday morning and phoned him three times in the evening. Otherwise he would never have come, since he tried to keep his nose out of other people's business, but he had to tell the *Madama* never to come back to the tavern. The problem was, none of this would remain secret for long; they were sure to learn of his connection to her sooner or later. Mr Lakatos arrived two days ago, and the *Madama* came in a taxi yesterday morning. If they knew that, they could question all the taxi drivers in the city until they came up with the Excelsior, or perhaps Lakatos himself would give them up under interrogation. *Chi lo sa?* The point was, one way or another they were sure to find us eventually.

In spite of everything, I found it hard to take any of this too seriously.

'But what does it matter if they arrest us? We're Hungarian citizens of good standing and we've got nothing to hide.'

'*Signore*, this is not that sort of thing at all. They will take the *Madama* Anderson to prison, and you too. It is a very quick thing to be arrested, and a very slow thing to persuade them afterwards that you are innocent. They will not pay the slightest attention to anything you say, but if your Embassy gets word and complains, or the people from your home… But that is a thing that takes many months. That is why I say to you, go now! Before they come for you!'

Milolu propped her chin on a long, slender finger and frowned pensively.

'Tell me, friend, what would be the point of trying to travel on? They can simply put out a warrant for our arrest and catch us on the road.'

'Better to try! Anything is better than staying here! So far you have not come up in the investigation; if they knew about you they would have questioned me about your visit yesterday. You might have a day or two until they find out about your connection to the arrested man. By then you could be across the border, or on some foreign ferry.'

Milolu thought for a moment.

'No, we can't just leave poor Lakatos in the lurch. That would be cowardly, especially since it was me who... No, I can't.'

Incensed, Pancia waved his arms in frustration.

'Understand, *Madama*, you cannot help him now. Nobody can! Do you understand?' It was plain that he wanted to shout, and only succeeded in moderating his voice with a considerable effort of will. 'If you get home you may be able to persuade important people to take up his case. Then there is a chance. The only possible result if you try to help him from here is that you will bring yourself and this gentleman into the biggest possible trouble!'

He rose and clumped across the floor on short legs. At the door he turned.

'I did what I can,' he said, 'and told you what I know. I can do nothing else. If they ask me about you then I will have to tell them the truth: that you were in my tavern and left together with Lakatos yesterday morning. If I tried to deny it I would end up in as much trouble as you, and that would be the end of me. I have to get back now; I have been gone too long already.'

He hurried off. I went after him, wanting to give him some token of thanks, but he was quicker than me. Instead of going down the grand staircase he ducked down the service stairs and I lost sight of him.

Well, this rather changes things: it seems we're in a bit of a pickle. Previously we had imagined we were only up against Schönberg and his gang, but now we can add to our list of potential adversaries the entire Italian state. Whether the situation is really quite as grave as the excitable Pancia claims is, in my opinion, still doubtful, but there can be no doubt at all as to his honesty. If he thought it important enough to risk visiting us here then the least we can do is take him seriously.

But none of it makes any damned sense! Milolu's best guess is that the thieves framed poor Lakatos so they could be rid of him. I'm inclined to agree—or at least I can't think of a better explanation—but for the life of me I can't imagine how they did it. He's not just anyone, after all, he's an official representative of the Budapest police force!

Madness!

Still, it's more crucial than ever that we make a definite decision now.

We debated our options. Clearly the safest thing was to leave at once, but how? The flight to Naples would not leave until morning, and it was risky even to ask the concierge downstairs about evening ferries. Anyone travelling abroad from Palermo has to register with the port authorities, and anyone leaving the country at such short notice is sure to attract attention. Milolu suggested that I go alone, though without much conviction; I had the impression she just didn't want me to think she was forcing me to stay in this difficult situation. I wouldn't hear of it, naturally. The very idea of making a run for it alone and leaving her to deal with this! I'll leave her later, of course—I shan't pretend my views on that point have altered—but a man needs at least one or two principles, and not abandoning a woman in danger is one I intend to stick to.

For the time being, we are in this mess together.

The easiest thing, we at last decided, would be to take the car. We'll leave our belongings at the Excelsior and say we want to tour the south and west of the island for a day or two. I've got a whole fictional itinerary in my head, from Trapani to Marsala, then to Selinunte and Agrigento before heading back to Palermo. We're off to see the Greek ruins, I'll say. Or would it be less conspicuous simply to leave without volunteering any plans? No, better to give them a destination. Trapani is eighty kilometres away; it will appear natural enough that we want to spend the night there. That's the direction we'll go, then take the turn-off for Messina; it's a good thing I've already driven all the roads around here! If we set off around seven, and if I drive fast we should be in Messina by ten or thereabouts, maybe even a little earlier. There are always ferries across the straits to the Italian mainland, and when we get there we can work out what to do next.

We can't leave before seven because Milolu wants to call her editorial office in Budapest and tell them what happened to Lakatos, and to ask them to do everything in their power to secure his immediate release. That should carry more weight than if she were to intervene directly, since they can apply continual pressure, while we don't know what would happen if we were to contact the authorities ourselves.

Messina, one in the morning
We did more or less as outlined above. I quickly packed whatever would fit in my overnight bag, then had the car trunk brought up to Milolu's room, since it's the only thing big enough for the painting. When I was ready I went down to the front desk and explained our plans—Trapani, Agrigento and all the rest of it—and said that since it was Wednesday and it wasn't absolutely certain we would be back before Saturday, which is the weekly payment day here, I would rather settle up for both myself and Milolu before I left.

I paid, and so far as I could tell aroused no suspicions. The concierge even gave me two or three little booklets with things to see in our various destinations, and particularly recommended the Grand Hotel in Trapani. I had, I thought, about as much likelihood of seeing the Grand Hotel Trapani as the dark side of the moon, but of course I thanked him warmly and said we'd be back by Sunday at the latest.

It's been quite a revelation, in fact, just how well I can lie when I have to. I dare say there are plenty of other 'honest men' who, in time of need, could pick up the knack of it with equal ease.

I filled the tank in the hotel garage, then drove the car round and parked in front of the entrance. Milolu, meanwhile, had quickly explained everything to her people in Budapest and was already waiting for me with her bags, and of course the all-important trunk. We had everything loaded and—after the obligatory round of tips—set off. I don't believe anyone gave us so much as a second glance; the hotel is always busy at that time of the evening.

We headed down the main road for a while, then turned right so as to get out of the city by the back streets. That way it was easier to check if anyone was tailing us. I was continually glancing in the rear-view mirror, and Milolu kept looking over her shoulder and asking if anyone was following us. No, there were no cars behind us. It was entirely dark by now, and we would certainly have seen headlights in the mirror.

Still, I couldn't help breathing a sigh of relief when we at last turned off the Monreale Road behind the royal palace and got onto the Corso Tukory—named after Lajos Tüköry, a Hungarian hero who fought with Garibaldi's Redshirts— which led us down to the Messina Road.

This stretch of road runs almost arrow-straight, allowing my little Lancia to pick up tremendous speed. Through the powerful beam of the headlights we saw trees and houses zip by, the speedometer hovering between a hundred and a hundred and twenty. It was a glorious feeling, a feeling of liberation. I'm not sure I've ever enjoyed any journey quite so much as that long drive down the coast road. The tarmac unfurled before us in a shimmering, moonlit ribbon, the sea glinting to our left beyond an endless border of blooming geraniums. White wave crests receded between the shore and the far horizon in an endlessly repeated dance, with the night air warm and sweetly fragrant around us. Milolu sat beside me, wide-eyed and happy, and neither of us said a word.

We drove on through the night as though my little car had wings.

13th of March, morning
In Messina, perhaps because I showed them my ENTE—the Italian visa card—and told them that Milolu was my wife, we weren't asked to show our passports. It isn't generally a requirement for domestic ferry travel. The next ferry doesn't sail until early in the morning, so we decided to check into a hotel. Since I've had no personal contact with Lakatos, it

seems prudent to do everything in my name where possible; we booked a single room for the two of us.

I awoke at dawn. The sun had not yet risen, but dull daylight already glimmered through the blinds.

I propped myself on one elbow and looked down at the woman lying next to me. She was sound asleep, her face turned towards me on the pillow, with thick black hair strewn about her as though blown by a gale. She was lying on her chest, her right arm crooked on the pillow in front of her, splayed fingers almost touching her nose.

I looked at her for a long time.

How different she seemed now! This was not the deliberate, resourceful, knowledgeable woman that I knew in her waking hours. Not the wily, independent schemer who had orchestrated the purchase of a stolen Leonardo da Vinci and weighed with such calm objectivity the mounting dangers that hedge us in. She looked entirely different now, with an innocence in repose that was almost childlike. Below her thick lashes I saw dark rings of exhaustion while her lips were slightly parted, as though breathing a silent prayer. There was a slight twist in the corner of her mouth, perhaps a sign of pain, and that hand raised as if in entreaty or supplication… What an affecting impression she made! In that moment she was—or so it seemed to me at least—as vulnerable as a little girl, pursued and tormented by some force far more powerful than herself, imploring mercy…

Nothing, not even drink, betrays our hidden selves quite like sleep. All the armour we gird ourselves in, the irony, the self-assurance, it all falls away, and our naked selves—perhaps our pasts too—stand in wordless testament to all the truth we bury.

I will confess, in other words, that I was moved; perhaps to excess. Could it have been merely a fond male fantasy to imagine her in that moment as weak, defenceless and alone, desperate for a strong arm to lean upon? I don't know, but I lay gazing at her for a very long time. At length, though, it was time to get up. Climbing gingerly out of bed, I began dressing as quietly as I could. Milolu did not wake, and so I stole silently from the room.

It was still just a little after six.

Later the same day
I'm writing these words on the lower deck of *La Bella Galatea*.

The first thing I wanted to do this morning was to find out precisely what our options were for onward travel. Was there a steamer? When did it leave? The ferry crosses the straits to Reggio Calabria fairly regularly, of course, but we both felt it would be safer to sail at least as far as Naples if a ship went early enough. It would be harder for Schönberg's gang to pursue us by boat, and we could sail as a married couple under my name. Nobody aboard would hear Milolu's real name and so the search for her would quickly hit a dead end.

I left the hotel and crossed the street, entering a small café where one or two other early risers were eating breakfast. The waiters both yawned continually and looked half asleep, but they brought my coffee willingly enough. That's something I've noticed about Italians, actually: hardly the most industrious of people, but very obliging.

I had just buttered my toast and was getting down to business with the marmalade when an unfamiliar voice greeted me in Hungarian. I turned to see a young man approaching my table. His hair was blonde, while his frame was so slender he seemed to have almost no shoulders at all. He smiled broadly.

'Do excuse me for interrupting your breakfast, Mr Vida; my mother always said I was an importunate little brat! The name's Endre Bodoki. I'm from Budapest and I dare say, *maestro*, that I'm among your most devoted admirers! That's why I couldn't help saying hello, even though you don't know me.'

'You know my work? How?'

'How do I...? Why, who could remain ignorant of a composer who has written so many timeless masterpieces? Your work is admired not only at home but also abroad, bringing prestige and renown to your homeland! *Shakuntala* is still being performed in London, with sell-out performances and rave reviews!'

I confess to feeling a certain pleasure at this breathless stream of compliments; I suppose all of us who work in the arts do so in hopes of praise. We're pleased if someone recognises us, and pleased to hear first-hand that our work has touched someone. Naturally we feign humility and make excuses—that's simple good manners—but inwardly we're like dogs with eagerly wagging tails.

I had resolved not to get to know anyone for as long as I was with Milolu, and that peculiar business with the chloroform has made me even more cautious than before, but I decided to make an exception for young Bodoki. What a vain creature I am!

I invited him to my table and asked him whether he was here on his honeymoon or just as a simple tourist. Had he been away from home long?

'Oh, ages!' he said. 'I've been living in Italy for a few years now. I graduated in Budapest, but you know what it's like there: crawling with graduates and no decent jobs! My mother grew up in Fiume when it was still Hungarian territory, though of course it's been part of Italy since the war, and a few relatives of hers managed to find me a job at the Fiat works in Turin. I've been employed there as a travelling salesman for the past few years. I won't pretend it's a dream come true, but it keeps me fed and watered. I've just come from Catania, heading back up north.'

A travelling salesman? Well, I thought, he'd surely know the routes through Italy as well as anyone. I explained to him that my wife and I were on our way back to Hungary and that I had risen so early in the morning to check whether there were ferries to Naples—so much more convenient than driving when the weather was as fine as today.

'You're absolutely right,' Bodoki said. 'I'm planning to go that way myself, in fact. It's not much slower than the train and about half the price. I don't suppose the cost matters much to a man like yourself, but it makes a great difference to me.'

He then offered to run straight down to the ferry boat offices and check the timetables for us.

'Just wait here. I can sort out everything and be back within an hour.'

This, however, I did not accept. True, it would have been pleasant to have another hour in the café, but I did not want this young man buying me tickets on a luxury liner where security would in all likelihood be tighter. What I wanted was the sort of downmarket little steamer that was generally used only by Italians themselves, but I would have struggled to explain my motives to a young man so in thrall to my worldly success. My refusal would itself have been difficult to explain, at least without a certain awkwardness, so I said I wanted a walk myself, and we strolled down to the harbour together.

Young Bodoki set about gathering information with remarkable eagerness, jogging here and there on fresh, youthful legs. Before I even had the chance to enter a single office he was back with news that only one ship would sail from here to Naples before noon, *La Bella Galatea*. It was not a passenger ferry of the sort that I had imagined, but rather a cargo vessel which also carried a small number of passengers.

We boarded it, and were shown a few simple but clean cabins, while there was also enough space on deck for my car. The only problem was the slowness of the crossing. It would take us sixteen hours to reach Naples, since it called at the Aeolian Islands first. All the same, I decided that was a price worth paying.

Whether in the ferry company offices or when talking to the sailors and captain of the vessel, Bodoki never failed to tell them all what a great man I was. His Italian was, in truth, a good deal worse than I would have expected from someone who had spent so much time in the country, but he made up for it with enthusiasm. I was not exactly thrilled to have my name and occupation so liberally broadcast— aside from anything else, such information always steeply hikes the expected tip—but I could do little to stop him. The ticket price was low, in any case, and the food was sure to be as good as it always is in Italy, even at sea.

We walked back to the hotel together, Bodoki to collect his luggage and I to tell Milolu of everything I had accomplished.

It was still only nine or so when I entered the room, where I found her already dressed and eating breakfast. She'd had it sent up to her room, not wanting to let the travelling case—where the Leonardo was stored amid a great mass of linen undergarments—out of her sight for an instant. I told her everything I had done that morning, and she seemed pleased enough. The only thing that made her frown was when I told her of young Bodoki and the way he made my acquaintance. She said nothing definite, but her voice was wary and suspicious.

'Who? From Budapest? What an odd coincidence!'

There was little time to chat, though, since everything had to be packed up and carried down to the Lancia. Then we drove to the harbour and handed it over to the longshoremen, who made sure it was secured in such a way that it would not slide across the deck in high seas. We left the painting in the car, deciding that this was the safest place for it. It is at the bottom of a locked travelling trunk, in a locked motor car with all the windows closed. Nobody can get to it since the car is in the middle of the deck and in clear view of both passengers and crew. The only things we brought to our cabin were our two little sponge bags, as well as a big plain eiderdown under which Milolu likes to sleep. That should be enough to tide us over until tomorrow morning.

At this final moment I was seized once more by anxiety. Would the authorities be alerted to our escape from Sicily at the last minute? Might a squadron of police cars wail down into the port in pursuit of Milolu? But no, nobody came. I felt soaring relief when the great motors began to thrum, the mooring lines were tossed ashore, and our vessel at last turned her prow towards the open sea.

The Aeolian Islands. A jumble of bare, ragged cliffs beneath largely extinct volcanoes. I say largely extinct, but as I write these words I am looking out at a slender plume of smoke rising from the cratered summit of Mt Stromboli. There's something curiously domestic about the scene, and I picture the volcano as a kindly old uncle puffing on his afternoon pipe. All the same, I heard someone say that Stromboli erupts more regularly even than Etna.

Bodoki remains as zealous as ever, the sole difference being that Milolu has replaced me as the object of his ardent devotion. As soon as we docked in the harbour of Lipari he raced into town, soon returning with a bouquet of peonies for her. He was also clutching a good-sized paper bag filled with some of the largest and juiciest strawberries I have ever seen. Strawberries! In the middle of March! It seems that warm winds off Africa mean there is practically no winter to speak of in these parts, and fruit ripens at the oddest times of year. In any case, he presented these gifts to Milolu in rather the manner I expect an ancient petitioner at Delphi might have laid his offerings before the statue of a revered deity. Alas, our poor pagan was disappointed: the goddess received these tributes with palpable coldness. Several times he offered to fetch his travelling rug so she might sit more comfortably, or to bring up one of the pillows from his cabin, but she unsmilingly shook her head.

The thing is, I know we've got to be careful and all that, but poor Bodoki's really not such a bad sort. This morning he said he had a headache and retired to his cabin, then did the same thing after lunch. If that was—as I suspect—discretion rather than illness, then he's rather more tactful than I gave him credit for.

Milolu and I are sitting on two deck chairs which we unfolded on the cargo deck right next to my car. The sea is as smooth as a lake and as strikingly, almost unnaturally blue as if we were sailing across some titan's cobalt drinking bowl. A deep, drowsy contentment has settled over me, and we sit next to one another in silence. There is something truly marvellous about our stately passage across a blue sea beneath a blue sky, with a spring breeze rippling through our clothes. Sometimes my hand seeks hers, sometimes hers mine, not from any sensual motive but simply for the deep contentment that touch can bring. The feeling is—dare I say it—almost akin to a honeymoon, and I'm as happy as if I were on one. Why should I deny it? No one but myself will ever read the words written here, and the truth is that when I saw her pained, girlish, innocent expression as she slept in bed this morning, it first occurred to me that I might feel something deeper than mere attraction and esteem for this woman. Not that I'm really in love with her, of course—I don't mean *that*—it's just that my feelings towards her have grown rather more complicated since I saw that hint of vulnerability in her this morning. I saw some part of her which she never shows when she's awake—but what is it? The truth is, I don't know. There was something desperate in it, something hunted, as though seeking support or refuge. In the end I'm forced to admit that I don't know the first thing about her, except that she's divorced. She lived in Chicago for a time then came back to Budapest, but it can hardly have been the comfortable life of a wealthy divorcee, since she surely wouldn't have taken a job as difficult as journalism if she didn't have to. That means she's probably poorer than she likes to pretend, and has nobody at all to support her financially. It also shows she has principles: in a city like Budapest a pretty, unattached young woman like her can always find a wealthy 'patron' to keep her in comfort if she doesn't mind feigning interest in elderly bankers or aristocrats.

Could she have escaped from a troubled, violent past? No, I can't quite see it being anything like that, but who knows? Who knows anything about women, for that matter? Looking out at the white wake stretching back southwards from beneath our stern, I feel at once a sudden similarity between women and the ocean: ships sail across the surface, leaving shallow marks behind, then a storm comes and blows away all trace, until you'd never know that any other ship had passed that way before. Not that it takes a storm, of course; the biggest ocean liner in the world can sail across a patch of ocean and within ten minutes it's as tranquil and undisturbed as any other spot, as vast, eternal and unreadable as it ever was, and ever shall be… I must be in a strange mood, because I can't get this thought out of my mind. Endless is the mystery of the trackless ocean, and endless the mystery of woman.

They're dashed attractive, though! It would be a fine thing if I could lose the habit of brooding and focus on what's in front of me. Who on earth cares what happened in her past? The main thing is that she's here now and she's mine. Every time I slip my arms around her I see her face light up, pleasure shining in those big brown eyes. Her mouth opens and she murmurs in that rich, smooth voice I already know so well. What more do I want? Can't I just enjoy these moments for what they are? Is this not a rich gift indeed, to have fallen into my lap by complete chance?

I repeat this thought to myself several times. I've lived long enough now to know that when something good happens in life, it's always wise to take conscious note and savour it to the full. We should pinch ourselves and say, 'Look, you ass, you're happy! Pay attention! Roll the film, so that later when it's gone you'll still have a precise, living record of it in your memory that you can keep forever.' That is especially true for me now, since I can hardly claim to be in the springtime of my years, with many a youthful adventure lying in store.

Just at the moment it doesn't even matter to me much that disappointment probably awaits. In fact, given the circumstances, a broken heart is a racing certainty at this point. Who knows what will happen with this strange, remarkable, entrancing woman? Who the devil cares?

She's here now, she seems to like me, and she is absurdly beautiful. Let tomorrow shift for itself.

Milolu—Milolu… What a fine choice I made in that sweet, sensual name.

VI

Naples, 14th of March
I don't think I've known this woman to do one predictable thing yet.

We stayed up on deck for a good while after dinner, but at length we went down to our cabin to get ready for bed. My compartment is separated from hers by a dividing panel, and when I had put on my slippers and pyjamas I decided to check if Milolu was ready for bed. Before I had time, however, she came into my compartment still fully dressed, a travelling rug under one arm and a headscarf pulled low over her forehead.

'What's this?' I asked. 'What's happened?'

'Nothing,' she smiled. 'I just wanted to ask if I might borrow the car keys. I've actually taken a notion that I might spend the night in the car; we're leaving so early tomorrow, and it's easier for me to wake up this way. In any case, it will be lovely to spend an hour or so looking out over the moonlit waves. It might be safer too… The painting, I mean. If I'm in the car I won't have to worry about someone breaking in and stealing it while we're asleep. I know I won't get an hour's sleep otherwise, always tossing and turning, and starting at the least little noise.'

'If you feel so strongly about it then I'd be happy to spend the night up there myself.'

'No! I wouldn't dream of ruining your sleep for some silly notion of mine. You get a good night's rest; you've been on your feet since dawn this morning.' She gave a quiet laugh. 'Anyway, I said first. That means I get dibs.'

'For Heaven's sake, darling, it's hellishly uncomfortable sleeping in a car.'

'Oh, don't worry, I did it heaps of times in America. I'll be just fine.'

I tried a few other arguments, but to no avail; her mind was made up. We walked up to the car together and I fiddled with the catch for a few minutes before succeeding in lowering one of the front seats. That meant at least that she was able to lie flat, and soon she was snuggled under her blanket in what did indeed appear to be tolerable comfort. Indeed, there was something so charming about her pretty face peeping out from under the cover that for an instant I was tempted to... Well, let's just say I was tempted to climb in beside her.

She was up before me the next morning. When the ship's horn sounded and I walked through to the dining room for breakfast I found her already sitting at our table, freshly washed and radiant.

'Did you sleep all right?' I asked.

'Well enough.'

I gave what might in retrospect have been a rather mocking smile.

'And was it worth a night in my little car?'

She laughed. 'I'm not sure about that, but there was one thing. Very late at night someone came over and tried the door handle…'

'Someone what? Who?'

'I don't know, but most likely it was just one of the on-duty sailors making sure the doors were locked. I couldn't see his face, of course, since the moon had long since set. All I caught was a glimpse of a figure, faintly outlined for a moment against the dark sky. He only tried once, then disappeared.'

Seeing my alarmed expression, she smiled and shrugged.

'Who knows? Maybe I dreamt the whole thing.'

She can be so sweet!

We ate a slice of toast each then went down to pack; the port of Naples was already in sight.

We decided not to put up here at all, but to have some breakfast at a hotel and then set off for Rome in the early afternoon. It's only two hundred and fifty kilometres from here, which shouldn't mean more than three or four hours driving. Less, perhaps. The *autostrade* they're building across this country are some of the best I've ever seen. If we were only going as far as Rome this evening, that meant we could spend a little time looking around Naples. Knowing Milolu's passion for art, I thought we might pay a visit to the National Archaeological Museum.

Bodoki recommended having the car looked over in a garage after such a long time on the deck of a ship. He knew of a good one and offered to take care of the servicing himself, but Milolu interrupted him.

'No need; the car was very thoroughly serviced in Messina.'

It must be her fears for the painting that made her lie like that; she knows as well as I do that the car stood in front of the hotel all night in Messina.

Bodoki said goodbye, telling us he had business to do in Naples, but then turned back after going a few yards, saying he could not leave without telling us one more time just how much he admired us both.

What a treasure trove that Archaeological Museum is! Normally a gallery full of paintings and statues does little for me, but how much more fun it was to look at them alongside someone as responsive and passionate as Milolu! It is interesting to look at her too, and see the almost reverential way she gazes upon a truly great work of art. Her expression is transfigured, and she speaks only in the faintest of whispers, as one habitually does on entering a cathedral. She stood with wide, pious eyes before Praxiteles' *Aphrodite*, the *Artemis of Ephesus* and even the *Running Diana*, though apparently this sculpture is a later Roman copy. (In fact it was my favourite. What creamy ivory thighs! There is something so seductive in those polished curves of skin and fabric.) We stayed until about lunchtime, and those few hours will always remain for me a happy memory.

Returning to the hotel, we found Bodoki waiting for us at the entrance with a bouquet of red roses.

'For you, ma'am. Pleasant scents for your journey.'

He had a present for me too: a fully updated road map of Italy. Handing it to me, he managed to stammer a diffident request.

'I—I was wondering... I don't know, it's probably jolly importunate of me even to ask, but there's a favour that I...'

Naturally enough, I encouraged him.

'By all means, young man. Just say the word!'

What he wanted was a lift as far as Rome. That would be a big saving for him, since I doubt the Fiat company pays him much. He seemed also to view the opportunity to spend a little more time with us as a blessing in itself. I paused, and he began telling me how many people he knew in Rome, which might be handy for us...

I glanced at Milolu. Women are always so much more adroit at saying 'no' in situations like this; I always make a fool of myself. Her response, though, was quite different from what I expected. Instead of refusing his request she smiled warmly at him and nodded.

'Of course, we'd be happy to take you with us! There should be plenty of room in the back seat.'

What an utterly unpredictable woman she is! Until now she's given every indication that she could not stand the sight of poor Bodoki, and now she's willingly taking him with us in the car. I don't believe I'll ever work her out.

Genzano di Roma, 14th of March
We reached this little place beside Lake Nemi at around five in the evening. At first we only planned to have a quick meal and stretch our legs, which after three and a half hours' driving was—in my case at least—sorely needed.

After eating we drank coffee on the restaurant terrace; I usually prefer tea in the afternoon, but except at the grandest hotels, the tea in Italy is almost always filthy.

We also had a marvellous view of the lake, which used to be the crater of an ancient volcano and thus forms an almost perfect circle. On the far side, where thick stands of oak run down to the lakeside, my Baedeker guide says there was once a temple to Diana. Might that be why the far shore is still so densely forested? The other three sides are nothing but scree and rocky escarpments.

There were only two of us, since Bodoki had gone off to telephone his company's offices in Rome. Milolu was silent, and though she looked out at the scenery I could tell that she was preoccupied by something else. At last she turned to me.

'Might it not be better to stay here for the night?'

'I'd be happy to, if you like. Any particular reason, besides how pretty the place is?'

'It is pretty, isn't it? I was thinking of something else, though: It seems to me we're safer in small places like this than in big cities. We're practically the only guests here, which means if somebody else arrives we're sure to notice them. It isn't like that in a big luxury hotel in the city.'

I was not a hard man to persuade, especially as I sensed that while she did not mention it explicitly, she was still troubled by the Lakatos case. If her name had come up in the investigation and the police were hunting for her, they would be less likely to come and search an out-of-the-way little place like this. Besides, it's not as though I needed an excuse for a quiet evening; a dawn start, a museum tour and a two-hundred-kilometre drive take a surprisingly heavy toll on a man of my age.

We took two rooms, and had the trunk brought up from the car. While Milolu put her clothes into the drawers, I slumped onto a sofa. My eyelids felt heavy.

'You won't come over and sit beside me?' I asked. 'There's plenty of room for two, and we could have a siesta. When almost in Rome and all that…'

She smiled. 'Not just now. Short naps never do me any good anyhow. No, I think I'll go for a walk instead, but you stay here and get some sleep.'

In a moment she was gone.

I awoke a little while later and had already gone down to the restaurant in anticipation of dinner when Milolu reappeared. I sensed at once that she was more excited than before; her eyes twinkled as though with some new and secret triumph. Striding over to me, she did not so much as say hello before asking an abrupt question.

'Where's Bodoki? He isn't with you?'

'Bodoki? No, I haven't seen him…'

She turned and left the room again, and I heard her voice out on the terrace.

'Mr Bodoki! Where are you? No, no, you must have dinner with us, I absolutely insist!'

I could not hear the young man's replies, only Milolu's voice.

'But you're our guest! Please let us at least treat you to dinner!'

At length they both appeared, but Bodoki could hardly have looked more unwilling if she had been dragging him on a leash. His normally solicitous manner was now exaggerated almost to the point of servility and he was as anxiously, forlornly eager to please as a beaten dog. Milolu, by contrast, was on top form, and hardly stopped talking the whole evening. She teased Bodoki constantly, and when dinner was finished she had a box of dominoes brought over. Bodoki wanted to leave, but she wouldn't hear of it.

'Come on, everyone knows how to play dominoes, and you need at least three for a game!'

His efforts to escape were futile; the three of us stayed at the table until at least eleven. I don't think I've ever seen Milolu in quite such high spirits, with such energy and humour… Still, behind that humour there was something else; how can I describe it? Some devilish delight in tormenting the scrawny young man in front of her. I don't believe she once took her eyes off him.

I had just written the above and got into my pyjamas when the door opened and Milolu came in. Her expression was quite changed now, no longer cheerful but serious and troubled.

'I have to tell you something very important,' she said.

And that it certainly was. Gave me no end of a shock, too. It turns out that while I was napping on the sofa, she had taken Bodoki for a walk. Then, sitting him down on a bench, she interrogated him closely. She had, she said, suspected from the first moment she met him that this young man was not all he claimed to be. For one thing, it struck her as very peculiar that a man who had lived in Italy for years and who had worked as a salesman for the Fiat motor company should have such a poor command of the Italian language. How would he ever sell anything, communicating in that ungrammatical babble? It also seemed strange to her that he should have recognised me so completely by chance in that little café in Messina. Then there was the business of the boat, and the shadowy figure who had tried to open the car door. She was practically sure, she said, that it had been Bodoki, but had not wished to worry me unnecessarily before now. Now, however, she was absolutely certain not only that he was the man, but also that he was part of Schönberg's gang. He had been sent to keep track of us and to report on our movements.

'But—how the blazes did you work that out?'

'I bluffed! Interrogated him! Squeezed him like a lemon! He finally admitted that Schönberg is waiting for us in Rome. I'll tell you the details later, but that's not the point now. The main thing is that we've got to get away from here, before he's able to tell anyone where we are. That's why I forced him to stay with us all evening, so he couldn't find some way of communicating our location. We've got to go now, though, in secret and without him, so we can finally shake them from our trail.'

'That's why you told him we'd only be leaving around lunchtime tomorrow?'

'Yes. I wanted him to think he would have time to phone Schönberg early tomorrow morning.'

After considering the situation, I have at length decided that she is right. Our safest course is to slip away at once, unnoticed. If we carry our things down to the car ourselves then we won't have to wake the porter. But where should we go? Rome is only twenty-something kilometres away, but we certainly can't stop there. We'll work something out, though; I'll take a look through the Baedeker when I have a free moment.

But first we have to get away! No time to lose!

Again we must briefly abandon the diary of Tibor Vida, for at no point in his writings does he describe what took place between Mrs Anderson and Endre Bodoki, and—as later events will show—their conversation was vitally important.

After leaving a drowsy Tibor slumped on the sofa, Milla went downstairs and found Bodoki sitting on the terrace.

'Won't you come for a stroll with me?' she asked. 'I'd enjoy the company, if you aren't too tired.'

The young man was only too eager to join her and they set off down the hillside together. After descending a long, uneven flight of steps they turned onto a little path, and came after about fifty paces to a wooden bench. Milolu stopped.

'Let's sit down for a minute. The view from here is simply wonderful…'

Sitting down, she smiled at Bodoki and patted the free space beside her. The sun had set but it was still light, and though the landscape before them was beginning to fade from vibrant colour to washed-out purples and greys, it was still possible to see a long way into the distance. The far line of the western horizon was still marked by a red glow where the sun had set, and the few ragged cirrus clouds had underbellies of salmon pink.

They looked out at the spellbinding evening landscape in silence for a few moments, then Milla turned to Bodoki. For another five or six seconds she did not speak, but her brown eyes were fixed on him with extraordinary intensity.

When at last she did speak, her voice was severe.

'I wonder if you wouldn't mind explaining, Mr Bodoki, precisely why you have decided not to tell us the truth about yourself?'

Clearly taken aback by this question, Bodoki was momentarily at a loss.

'I—well, I mean—look, I—I certainly wouldn't…'

'Oh yes you would. You told us you came from Catania. That was a lie, wasn't it?'

'Please, I swear, I…'

Milla smiled, taking two torn strips of paper from her handbag. It was a hotel receipt.

'You see this? It's your hotel receipt from Palermo, dated the twelfth of March. Remember when you got off the boat in Lipari to buy me those flowers and strawberries? Well, that's when I took a look around your cabin, the same way you looked round mine that same morning.'

'I—what? Never! I…'

'Don't be silly, of course you did. I even know what you rummaged through. Remember my travelling blanket with the leather straps? I know you unbuckled it to see if I had hidden anything inside. You didn't take anything, but you didn't fold it up again the way I do. That was careless, Bodoki. There's something else, though. During the night you tried to open the car door, but it was locked. I was the one who locked it, but from inside. I was in the car, you see, and I recognised you.'

'I—no, you've got it all wrong. I—I couldn't sleep with the headache I had, so I went for a stroll on deck. Then—I don't know, I was just curious. I suppose I may have put a hand on the latch…'

Mrs Anderson fixed Bodoki with a more balefully menacing expression than he had ever imagined possible on her pretty face, and seeing his alarm, she grew bolder.

'Shall I tell you who you are? Not your real name, since I admit I probably don't know that yet, but shall I tell you what you do and why you've attached yourself to us in this way? Shall I?'

Unable to answer, Bodoki just stared at her.

'But I don't need to go into all the details, do I? One name should be enough: Schönberg.'

'Schönberg…?'

'Yes, Mr Schönberg-Belmonte, to give him his full honorific. Know the name? I certainly do. I've done business with the man, or at least I would have done if I'd accepted the offer he made me. Now admit it: Schönberg sent you after us. Admit it!'

'Ma'am, I'm sorry, but I truly don't have the faintest idea… I've never heard of him, and I don't understand what's going on!'

'Don't be ridiculous, you know perfectly well what I'm talking about, and this gaping and babbling just proves it.'

They were both silent for a moment, but when Milla resumed speaking her voice was more threatening than ever.

'Tell me, what do you think would happen if I were to tell Mr Schönberg how carelessly you've handled your mission? How would you expect him to react? I could tell him about finding the Palermo receipt in your bags, which you only had to toss overboard at a convenient moment, or about your absurd cover story. How did you expect anyone to believe you work as a salesman here when you barely speak Italian?' Her tone was scornful and mocking. 'I could tell him all that and more, so perhaps you should stop this childish nonsense and tell me the truth.'

'Please, miss—I mean ma'am—I… Please don't tell him…'

'Well,' she said, then raised a hand. 'No, hold on a minute. I haven't finished.'

She was silent for a few moments while Bodoki wiped his forehead with a handkerchief. She was thinking about what she had heard from the Budapest police long before her departure for Italy. The Museum porter had described the 'painter's assistant' who stole the Leonardo as a slim young man with narrow shoulders and blonde hair. Bodoki fit perfectly. This was hardly conclusive, but instinctively she felt certain—almost as certain as if she had been in the Museum with him—that this young man was the thief.

'Yes, there's more,' she said, making sure her expression would not betray her before attempting another bluff. 'I know you were the young painter's assistant in the Budapest Museum.'

'Me? I…'

'Yes, you.' She jabbed a forefinger towards him like a dagger. 'All I have to do is call the Hungarian consulate and you'll spend the rest of your miserable life in prison.'

At this, the last of the frightened young man's composure finally crumpled; throwing himself to the ground in front of her, he took her hands in his and began imploring her.

'Please don't! Please, I'm begging you, don't! You don't know what a lot of trouble I'm in—I had no choice! I'm begging you! Look, you've already got the picture. Keep it! It's yours! But don't ruin a poor man's life!'

He pleaded in this way for a long time, no longer wiping the beads of sweat from his forehead but letting them trickle down his face in rivulets. She just watched him with glittering eyes, drinking in every detail of his despair with merciless delight. Looking up at her, Bodoki must have seen in her something akin to what the cornered mouse sees when it looks for pity in the eyes of a cat.

No, Milla Anderson felt no pity, only triumph and savage joy.

While Bodoki continued to beg at her feet, she considered what was to be done next. Report him? No, that would never work. She had no proof, and who would take her word for it? Bodoki would deny everything, or Schönberg's gang would help him disappear, then pursue Tibor and her with more fury than ever. No, reporting him could come later, perhaps, but not yet. The main thing now was to keep out of Schönberg's clutches, to win themselves some time so they could get out of Italy and reach the Hungarian frontier. These thoughts flashed through her mind in an instant, and she made her decision just as quickly.

'Well, all right then. I'll say nothing for now, but only on one condition: you tell me where Schönberg is.'

'Please, I can't! He'd kill me…'

'You won't tell me? You dare…' She stopped. Perhaps that was the wrong tone. Her voice shifted slightly. 'Listen, Bodoki, I know it's not your fault, and I'd never report you if there was another way. I've got to know where Schönberg is, though, and if you don't tell me then I'll have no choice…'

The young man began to sob, but between his gasps a single, almost whispered word emerged:

'Rome.'

So, she thought, he's leapfrogged us. He must have taken a plane.

Her voice rose again.

'So he's in Rome, is he? Well, I'll entrust you with a message. Tell him that the only way to get the painting is through me. And tell him that I'm still open to a deal if he doesn't attempt any more stunts of this sort. Tell him that, if you see him tomorrow.'

Relieved, Bodoki stammered his thanks.

'I—of course, only too happy. Just as you say…'

'Good. Let's leave it there, then. In any case, it must be almost dinner time by now and I'm famished. Shall we head back to the hotel?'

They walked back up the steps in silence, the woman triumphant and the man behind her like a whipped animal.

From the Diary of Tibor Vida

Viterbo, 15th of March, morning

We drove through Rome without stopping, and kept going until we reached the little town of Viterbo. Here we checked into a rather seedy, run-down little *albergo*, but there doesn't seem to be any better establishment in the town. It took a lot of ringing and knocking at the door before someone finally let us in; everybody must have been asleep. At last someone came to the door and we were able to get a room for the night. I couldn't go to bed immediately, though, since I had to do something about the car. There's no garage here, so I parked it in a narrow side-street. I can't leave it out on the main square in front of the hotel, since my Hungarian number plate is probably our biggest danger at this point. There are plenty of Lancias of my sort here in Italy, but there can't be more than one or two with Hungarian plates. Bodoki, in any case, must surely have noted down the number. They'll be hunting everywhere for us, and since it isn't hard to guess which general direction we need to head in, that narrows the search considerably.

It was a little after two when we decided to stop here. The truth is I could barely keep my eyes open; I was already tired from the two hundred kilometres to Genzano, and another hundred and sixty or so by headlights was about as much as I could take. All the same, I woke fairly early this morning. Milolu is still asleep as I write this; poor thing, she must have been exhausted.

Should I wake her? The truth is we really ought to get a move on and make the most of our time before they catch up with us.

What a stroke of luck I parked the car in an out of the way place and that we didn't set off sooner! I was shaving by the reflection in the window—there's no mirror in our room—when I saw a big touring car drive into town on the road from Rome and turn into the piazza. It was a big convertible in tulip red with a black canvas roof, and it was going conspicuously slowly. How many were inside I can't say for sure, but I saw the two men in the front seat clearly enough. One was Schönberg himself, the other the athletic young man who knocked me out with chloroform in Palermo. Both were leaning out of the window and looking at all the parked cars, driving slowly until they reached the far end of the square. Then I heard the motor rev as they sped off northwards.

They were looking for us; that's why they drove through the town so slowly! If we had already been on the road they would certainly have overtaken us, and what they would have done then is anyone's guess!

It's good that they didn't see us, but it's a problem that they're ahead of us again. What should we do now? Change direction? Milolu and I spent a long time debating our options.

Essentially, there are two possible courses of action. One is to go back the way we came, almost as far as Rome, then take the Ancona road; the other is to keep going towards Florence. Both are risky, but in the end we chose the latter. Going by Ancona would cost us a lot of time, and since both roads end in Bologna it wouldn't necessarily prove much safer. After all, when they don't find us on the road they're likely to wait for us in Bologna, since we have to pass that way anyhow.

Bologna, that's where the danger lies!

If only I didn't have these damned Hungarian number plates I wouldn't be so nervous! If I could get rid of them then we might just slip by under their noses.

Florence, the same afternoon
I managed to swap our number plates! Not only that, but I did it in just about the neatest, simplest way imaginable, severing the Gordian knot with a single cut!

It preyed on my mind during the whole of the long drive up from Viterbo. Two plates of white tin, with the number embossed in black characters, on both the front and back of my car. They would betray us at once to anyone who knew what they were looking for. What's worse, if we need to get the car repaired it's the easiest thing in the world to call round the local garages and ask if there are any Hungarian cars being serviced. If the fascists are really after Milolu then they could find out within a few minutes, and I doubt it would take Schönberg's gang much longer.

Nobody sells number plates, of course, or at least not legally, and I'm hardly the sort of fellow who can turn to his international underworld connections. I thought about painting over them, but the kind of smooth tin they use is designed to make that impossible without specialist equipment.

Still, I managed it! A set of Italian plates are now stuck to the front of my car.

We reached Florence late this morning, visited the Uffizi galleries around noon, then parted company for a few hours after lunch. Milolu wanted to visit the Pitti Palace, and though I was disappointed not to be able to go there with her, I had more important things to do.

First I went into a *papeteria*. (What a language! *Papeteria!* Saying a word like that out loud seems to call for a trumpet fanfare—*dov'è la papetepapeteria!*—and I can't help waving my arms about like a lunatic, but it's really nothing but a stationery supply shop.) I bought a couple of sheets of white and jet-black paper, as well as some tracing paper, a short ruler and a tub of strong glue. Returning to the hotel garage, I knelt down beside an Italian car and traced the oval-shaped disc on the left of the number plate where the car's nationality is indicated, as well as the number one. Then, going back up to our room, I set to work. First I cut out two circles of white paper which would cover the 'H' for Hungary, then a black 'I' for Italy which I would superimpose on top. The original number plate is long and narrow, with U 23 196 on it. Number one being the easiest to cut out, I made a couple of number ones and stuck them on white backgrounds cut out to fit them. I also wanted to replace the U at the beginning with an X, but this proved more difficult; after a couple of failed attempts I at last managed something I decided was close enough to the real thing to pass. Then I went back to the garage (deserted, thankfully) and began sticking the false letters to the plates. After sticking them on I covered both plates with a thick layer of the transparent glue, giving the plates an enamel sheen I judge virtually indistinguishable from the metallic originals. It looks marvellous! Now instead of being U 23 196 our plates read X 21 191, and with the all-important Italian 'I' on the left-hand side. What the X means I have no idea, but I've seen it often enough on cars here. Now our identities should be harder to establish from our car, and we'll look like locals. As soon as we reach the border I'll give it a good scrub with hot, soapy water and it should come off quickly enough, but for now I'm much happier with them as they are. The bright white paper matches the white tin background perfectly, and even if you look at it very closely it's almost impossible to see that it isn't genuine.

I can hardly express how pleased I am with my little piece of improvisation; I could hardly be more satisfied with myself if I'd painted that *Head of Christ* myself, and not Leonardo!

I was pleased too when Milolu came back and I could show her my handiwork. She praised it, but added that we'll have to drive more carefully than ever now; if we ever run into difficulties with the police and they discover what I've done we'll certainly be in hot water.

I reassured her, saying that I was hardly a hot-headed young racer. I keep to the speed limit and obey the Highway Code. Besides, I've always been a naturally cautious driver; it's not just my own driving I pay attention to—that goes without saying—but that of other cars on the road as well. Particularly when the road is wet or visibility is reduced, you have to keep your wits about you and notice when another man seems tired, or drunk, or simply a beginner, and give him more space than you normally would.

It's such a relief to have this new identity for our car, which should help us pass undetected through Italy. All being well, we'll be through Bologna by tomorrow evening.

I'm certain my little gamble was worth the risk.

VII

Padua, 16th of March, afternoon

I can't believe it, we've been arrested! We were picked up at a toll point and now we're at the local *carabinieri* station, me in one cell and Milolu in another. A guard is standing in the corridor to make sure we don't communicate with one another.

First I thought it was some kind of misunderstanding. I identified myself, and Milolu too. They replied that we were precisely the people they had been tasked with arresting. I asked what the grounds were and they said they didn't know. They say they're preparing a report and that until they receive instructions they won't allow us to communicate. So far there hasn't been any interrogation whatsoever, and I must say they've been remarkably polite about the whole thing.

They even brought us lunch from a little *osteria* across the street.

The fact is, though, I can't eat a bite. This whole day has been the most awful, miserable experience of my life. Not just because of the arrest, but because the business with the number plates, which I was so proud of yesterday, proved utterly useless! Not only that, but now they are another possible charge hanging over us. What a stupid thing to do! In any case, if I'm obliged to sit here killing time then I may as well write down what happened.

We left Florence yesterday evening, and spent the night in another run-down little roadside *albergo*.

We set off again this morning and within two hours we were through Bologna. We saw nothing suspicious, and fifty kilometres later we passed through Ferrara with equally little fuss. I didn't see anyone acting strangely, or obviously on the look-out for something. It must have been there that someone spotted us, though, or perhaps later in Rovigo. How? Perhaps they saw our faces and didn't even look at the number plates. Who knows? I certainly don't.

During the drive I kept glancing obsessively in the rear-view mirror. Nobody was following us; there wasn't a single car behind us. Then, when we got onto the long, straight stretch of road which runs parallel to the railway line all the way to Padua, I looked in the mirror again and I saw them! It was that big, tulip-red touring car with the black front grille, the same car I had seen driving through Viterbo with Schönberg in the passenger seat the morning before. It came careening out of a side-road, righted itself, and sped forward.

They were after us!

I put my foot down and we lurched forward. My light Lancia is a nimble machine, with good acceleration, and the distance between the two cars quickly increased; at one point we might have been three or four kilometres in front, but they soon began to close again. More people in their car must have slowed their acceleration, but that big touring car could pick up terrific speed on a long straight.

A contest began between my little sports car and their bigger vehicle. For my own part I just gripped the steering wheel with white knuckles and kept my foot firmly planted on the accelerator.

If the car pursuing us had been less heavily laden then I don't doubt they would soon have caught us, but there must have been five or six people in it, and only two of us. They still closed the gap between us, but only slowly. My poor little Lancia's speedometer hovered between a hundred and twenty and a hundred and twenty-five, and I watched our enemies draw steadily closer along that endless stretch of straight road. There was something nightmarish and unreal about it all; the flat countryside around us remained perpetually the same, and when being pursued one finds that any speed, however blistering, feels like a crawl. How I wished my little car could sprout wings and soar up over the endless, featureless floodplain of the Po!

I wished in vain, though, and still the bigger car drew steadily nearer. They were just a hundred metres or so behind us now, and I could already make out the figure of Schönberg sitting in the front seat, and even the dark strip of diagonal cloth which I knew to be the sling on his arm.

An express train came barrelling down the tracks which ran parallel to our road, heading like us towards Padua. Passengers looking out of the windows clapped and cheered when they saw us, then they too seemed to notice the furious pursuit which was underway. They leaned out of the windows, pointing both at us and at the car behind us, and even across the whine of our engine and the din of the locomotive I could hear their whistles and shouts.

We sped on.

A little way ahead we at last came to a bend, and I realised that our road led across the tracks. In the same instant I saw the barriers at the level crossing beginning to drop, and heard the ringing of the bell. In what was and will surely remain the most reckless driving manoeuvre of my entire life we skidded round the bend without losing speed and thumped spine-jarringly across the tracks. Had we struck the descending barriers we might have spun sideways across the tracks, just in time to be crushed beneath the oncoming locomotive! Had we braked and slowed, on the other hand, Schönberg and his henchmen would have been on us in an instant.

We made it! Thank God this car sits fairly low to the road; I think the barriers would have clipped the roof as they came down otherwise. But we were saved! Our pursuers would have to stop until the train had passed and the barrier lifted, while we could fly on as fast as this car would carry us! That delay, I thought, might give us just enough time to vanish once more.

Padua wasn't far off! We could already see the church spires and factory chimneys rising at the end of that arrow-straight road. And there was further cause for joy: another train—this time a freight locomotive pulling endless wagons—was chugging slowly down the tracks in the opposite direction, meaning the crossing would remain shut for much longer.

At such times, I have discovered, the brain works rather more quickly than usual, and I impulsively decided to turn left when we got into Padua, heading out west for a time. We would do as the hare does when fleeing the greyhound: zigzag wildly in hopes of throwing our pursuers with a sudden change of direction. Schönberg, I supposed, would tear straight through Padua and out onto the long *autostrada* towards Venice.

At that moment I felt new confidence welling within me! We passed the first houses on the outskirts of Padua, then the city's toll building. In front of it stood three tall, broad-shouldered *carabinieri* in dark-blue uniforms, looking like three exclamation marks. Their triangular white hats blocked the road, and the central figure raised a hand.

I slowed and stopped.

They asked to see our visas and our passports, and after glancing through them they officially informed us that we were being placed under arrest and would have to stay in the station until further notice.

I fumed, explained, cajoled and pleaded, but to no avail.

'*Abbiamo ordini*,' one man said with a very Italian shrug. 'We have orders.'

Our car was driven into the parking area while we were escorted towards the building. Glancing back, I saw

Schönberg's car tear past at breakneck speed. He was free, while we were imprisoned!

My word, what a mess!

It's not myself I'm principally worried about, of course, since it will soon become clear that I don't have the slightest connection to the Lakatos case. I never met him, nor indeed do I even know what the poor man looks like, and my rather amateur attempts to alter our number plates can't be so serious as all that. Perhaps they won't even notice, but if they do, what could the maximum penalty be for a little thing like that? A fine of a few hundred lire and a slap on the wrist, probably. I'm certain in Hungary it's only classed as a misdemeanour rather than a crime. Even if it turns out to be more—a few thousand lire, say, and the impounding of my car—it's still nothing compared to what poor Milolu could be facing.

Milolu—good God, what a mess! Milolu! They could threaten her with conspiracy against the state, or keep her in prison without charges for months, the way that little man in Palermo warned. It could be months and months and months before we're able to free her!

I feel faint and nauseous at the very thought.

I've heard so many horror stories about the fascists' prisons, and whispers about a secret island where political enemies disappear permanently, never to return. Do they really torture people here to extract confessions? If even half of what I've heard is true then it's hell on earth!

Oh Milolu, my sweet, sweet angel… How will I see you again? I can't even picture her face!

Afternoon, four o'clock
We've been transferred to the city prison, and of course we still aren't allowed to communicate. I've tried asking questions, but they won't tell me anything, not even where Milolu is being kept. Nothing.

They've taken my money and my chequebook. They gave me a receipt for them, but how much use that is remains to be seen. I've been left my sponge bag and this diary. They hardly looked at the diary, in fact; my passport describes my occupation as 'writer and opera composer' so I suppose they may assume it's some literary effort.

My cell is probably no different from any other prison cell in this country. A straw-stuffed mattress sits on top of a plank bed, and there are two wooden chairs beside a little desk. I was relieved to discover a flush toilet and a working washbasin as well.

What more do I need?

Only one thing, really. To know that Milolu is safe. This is the only thought that preoccupies me, and the endless uncertainty is driving me mad!

Evening, 8 o'clock
They've just brought me back to my cell after my first interrogation. I admit that I was more than a trifle nervous

as they led me there, especially since I met Milolu coming the other way, led like me by two guards. They must have interviewed her just before me, and I felt a fresh stab of pain as I considered that she was the prime suspect. We weren't permitted to stop and chat, of course, but as she passed me she flashed a smile and said, 'Don't worry, it'll turn out all right.' What a woman! Even in the midst of all this she still thinks to try and lift my spirits!

The police chief was precisely the sort of tall, thin, unsmiling man who, back when I was at school, always made my heart sink when I found out that he was to be my teacher. His nose was as narrow and hooked as a pruning knife, while the skin on his face was sallow and waxy. I wondered—inwardly—if there was perhaps something the matter with his liver. He was dressed in a black shirt, with a revolver holstered in a black leather shoulder harness. Anyone, I thought, who feels the need to carry a gun while sitting in his own office—and with two guards in the room—is a pretty gutless sort of a man.

The interview began with a peculiar question; he did not ask about Milolu, but about Bodoki. He asked where we first met him, and I said that he introduced himself in Messina; before that I'd had no idea he so much as existed.

The policeman noted this down, shaking his head as though in disbelief. Then he looked up.

'If he was a total stranger, why did you take him with you on the drive from Naples?'

'Only as a favour. He asked for a lift, and I saw no reason to refuse.'

Then he asked why we had travelled across Italy at such speed; what was the rush?

Not wanting to mention Schönberg, since after all we had not the slightest proof he was after us, I instead said that I was heading home on account of urgent business in Budapest. Thinking it might help if I explained who I was, I told him that I was a rather well-regarded opera composer who had enjoyed considerable success with one or two pieces, most notably *Shakuntala*, which had enjoyed a run of two hundred performances in London's West End.

The police chief raised an eyebrow.

'A run of two hundred shows? You want me to believe that? *Signore*, if that were true you would be a man of very substantial means, and would not have descended to the sort of criminality you stand accused of.'

'Me? Accused? What have I been accused of?'

'That, I think, is something you know perfectly well yourself.'

He went on to say that since I had been arrested, and had no hope of ever being released except through full cooperation, he advised me to confess everything honestly.

What was I to confess? I thought the man had perhaps lost his mind, or confused me with someone else entirely, so I repeated—a little louder this time—my name and social status. He turned that great, hooked nose towards me as though wishing to hang me from it, then began to shout.

'Your situation is extremely serious! The only way you will even get out of here is by confessing! Confess!'

This command was inexplicable, and I felt anger begin to rise in me.

'The most fundamental right of a prisoner in custody is to know the crime with which he is charged!' I said, my voice also rising.

'Silence!' he roared, but then pushed his chair back a few inches and began rummaging through the stack of documents in front of him. This went on for a few minutes, then he looked up again.

'How long have you known Mrs Anderson?'

I told him we met in Palermo, and he nodded as though this was the correct answer. After another few minutes spent sifting through the papers on his desk, he spoke to me in a curt, peremptory tone.

'And would you mind telling me why you falsified your registration plates? Why would an innocent opera composer do such a thing?'

It was, I see now, extremely stupid of me not to have prepared an answer to this question in advance, but ever since our arrest I had been so preoccupied with worries about Milolu. All I could think about was how to save her, and everything just slipped my mind. I had to think of some plausible excuse, and quickly; the hook-nosed investigator was already impatiently repeating his question.

'Well? Why? Why did you glue false numbers to your plates? Answer me!'

My mind momentarily went blank, and all I could do was numbly repeat his words.

'Glued...? Glued on...?'

'Yes. Glued on. Extremely skilfully, in fact, which shows that you are an experienced criminal. If we had looked only at the number plate then you might have succeeded in making your escape, but we are not such fools as that! I gave orders that every car of that particular make was to be stopped and searched. Now, tell me, why did you falsify the plates?'

I hesitated for a moment, but there was nothing for it; I had to tell him about the whole Schönberg story, since no lie concocted on the spot would survive for long. Anything implicating Milolu would have to be concealed, but I could no longer avoid speaking about Schönberg and his gang. This, I hoped, would at least explain why I falsified the number plates, though it would not of course make it legal.

So I told him almost everything, leaving out only Milolu's role in the purchase of the painting. As the story went on I said less and less about her, and of course I never once brought up Lakatos. The rest, however, I explained in as much detail as I could, starting with the auction. I told him about the Marquis Bentiruba and the tousle-haired man, about Schönberg's visit and the incident with the chloroform.

I also explained that they had pursued us across Italy, that I had seen them drive across the square in Viterbo and that they had been right behind us when we were arrested. I talked for a very long time, and through it all the hook-nosed policeman just watched me with a mocking smile. When I finished there was silence for a few moments, then he spoke.

'That's a very pretty story to come up with on the spot. I see you have imagination, at least. What did you call this dastardly nemesis of yours?'

'Schönberg-Belmonte. He stayed at the Villa Igea in Palermo. Ask them, if you like.'

'Certainly we will ask, though I don't believe a word of what you just told me. In any case, perhaps you have simply obtained the identity of some poor traveller who has not the slightest connection to your schemes, and are trying to pin the blame on him.'

This was just about as much sneering as I could tolerate. I banged on the desk and began to shout.

'I am not a liar! What I say is the whole, unvarnished and absolute truth!'

My sudden outburst seemed to startle him, for he stood up and took a step or two backwards. Still, he evidently enjoyed sneering too much to abandon the habit now.

'Really? You never lie? And didn't you just tell me you lied when you left Palermo? I want no more tantrums of that sort, and sit further back from the table or I will call the guards back in.'

I pushed my chair back, and he sat down again.

'You say you bought this painting. Where is it? And where is your proof of purchase?'

'The painting is at the bottom of a trunk in the boot of my car, and the receipt…'

I rummaged through my pockets, but couldn't find it. Of course I couldn't: I gave it to Milolu at the same time I gave her the painting, but in the consternation of the moment I didn't think of that.

'Hang on, just a second, it'll be in my papers…' I muttered, turning myself inside out.

This pantomime seemed to cheer my interrogator, and he allowed himself a little grin as he watched me.

'I have known all along that you do not have it,' he said, shaking his head. 'Now tell me, what is the point of making a fool of yourself like this? Admit that you have the Leonardo because you stole it from the Budapest Museum. I will ask you again, what is the point of all these lies? Why not just admit that you are the leader of the gang that stole the painting? What is the point of inventing all these outlandish characters, this "Marquis", "Schönberg", and that absurd fantasy about the chloroform? What's the point of wasting our time like this? We understand the situation very clearly, and you certainly are not going to escape from me with stupid inventions of this sort. I see precisely what happened, and it will all be a lot simpler and less uncomfortable if you simply confess the truth now. Confess! If you do I can send you on to Hungary, and the whole affair will be much more pleasant for both of us.'

'But I swear to you, you're wrong! I bought the painting!'

'It's no use lying to me!'

I was by now speechless with rage, and in any case had no idea what to say. I'm not entirely sure, but perhaps I threatened him again, and struck the table once more with my fist. The sallow-faced man leapt up again, and this time rang the bell. Two guards appeared at once.

'Take him away!' he shouted, 'and give him nothing but bread and water! I'll teach him how a prisoner behaves around here!'

As they led me back to my cell I felt again the curious, unreal sensation that this was a waking nightmare. And what about Milolu? What will become of her?

Dear God, what a mess we're in! And it's all my fault! I'm the one who got us both into this, and they're going to see her as the worst sort of criminal!

Her!

What are we going to do?

Here we must again leave the diary of Tibor Vida and acquaint the reader with events elsewhere. That means going back a bit.

As soon as it had been ascertained that the painting found in a suitcase at Keleti railway station was in fact a forgery, telegrams and phone calls were made to all border checkpoints asking for the names of everyone who had crossed the border that day, which is to say the twentieth of January. There were, of course, thousands of names, but only one attracted the interest of investigators. A certain individual by the name of Endre Bodoki had travelled west on that day aboard the Vienna Express, claiming to be a twenty-eight-year-old unemployed clerk, but with characteristics closely matching the description of the 'painter's assistant' who had stolen the Leonardo. Towards the end of the previous year he had applied for a passport, showing to the issuing authority papers proving that he had been offered gainful employment in Italy. At the beginning of January he received a passport authorising him to travel to Italy by way of Yugoslavia. This, of course, was scant enough evidence, and the investigators pursued it with little hope of real success; there were simply no other leads to follow. Who was this Bodoki, and where were his previous places of residence? No hotel, guest house or renting authority seemed to have heard of him.

There was not the slightest scrap of evidence and it is likely that the investigators would soon have given up in frustration if another and much more interesting piece of information had not come to their attention.

At the end of February an old lady from Munkácsy Street, the widow of the painter Péter Kilén, sought to bring a case before the local magistrates. Shortly after her husband's death she had decided to rent out his studio, and at last found a willing tenant in Endre Bodoki. He was not, curiously enough, a painter at all, but rather a clerk, and paid the first month's rent only in fits and starts. Then on the second of December he paid the next four months' rent in advance, but disappeared with all his personal effects in the middle of January. She had heard nothing from him since. What she wanted to know was this: seeing as the workshop was presently empty, could she rent it out to someone else, or would she have to wait until the lease to Bodoki expired at the end of March? She had a new tenant lined up to rent the space, and it seemed an awful waste to leave it unoccupied.

Well, this was news. The detectives immediately rushed over to speak with this old widow. From her they learned that Bodoki had not been alone when he rented the studio from the middle of December to the middle of January, but had shared it with a friend of his. Who he was she had no idea, of course, but whoever he was he was a 'queer sort of fish' who never went out during the daytime, and only occasionally at night. Lunch was always brought to him from the little place across the street. It was beginning to look more and more as though this was their mystery forger, since on one occasion when the door chanced to be open Mrs Kilén saw her husband's old easel set up next to the workshop window, with a few glass jars and tubes of paint on the table beside it. It was clear that Bodoki himself could not have been the painter, since he was only ever there at irregular intervals.

Whether this painter had left together with Bodoki or separately remained unknown, but they suspected that he had left a day or two earlier; the border report stated that Bodoki had been alone on the train, with just a small travelling valise.

The old widow's description of Bodoki matched the passport summary perfectly: a thin, blonde man with almost no shoulders at all, and at most thirty years of age. It now seemed increasingly likely that he had some connection to the theft.

They asked old Mrs Kilén if any other visitors had come to the workshop, but she said she had no idea; there were two entrances to the studio, one from her front room and one from the stairway, so it was perfectly possible for people to come and go without her knowledge.

The Budapest police hurried to share this new information with their counterparts abroad. Letters were sent to Yugoslavia, Austria and Italy, and within five or six days it was confirmed that Bodoki had rapidly crossed Austria and northern Yugoslavia, entering Italy at Postumia. This information was received after Lakatos's departure for Italy, so the remaining detectives relied on the postal service for communication with Rome. They sent copies of all the relevant documents and asked the Italian police to ascertain Bodoki's whereabouts. The parcel was sent by airmail, and by the eleventh of March it had already reached Rome.

The Italian police headquarters immediately issued a nationwide warrant for Bodoki's arrest, and the next day they received the news about Lakatos from the station in

Palermo. One day after that they received an even more urgent telegram from Budapest, protesting Lakatos's innocence and requesting his immediate release.

This, however, the Italians were by no means inclined to grant, since as far as they were concerned, the evidence of his complicity in an anti-fascist plot was overwhelming. His being, as it turned out, an actual Hungarian policeman was neither here nor there. If he was in fact Lakatos then he was simply using the pretext of official business to conduct his own nefarious affairs, and if his true identity was the Czechoslovak Novák then he had evidently worked to double-cross the Hungarians as well as themselves. Had the man in their custody perhaps murdered the real Lakatos and stolen his identity? They certainly would not put it past a Czechoslovak anti-fascist. The whole affair, in any event, demanded long and careful scrutiny; there was no question of simply letting the man go free. Indeed, Hungarian protestations only served to deepen their conviction that this Lakatos fellow was at the centre of some sinister international plot.

Still, they set considerable store by their good relationship with the Hungarian police force, so they made the search for Bodoki a priority, hoping that if they acquiesced in this favour, their non-committal response to requests for Lakatos's release would not be taken too badly. Orders were sent to police forces up and down the country, instructing them to seek out and apprehend Bodoki as a matter of urgency.

On the thirteenth of March it was established that he had been in Palermo until the evening before, and had then travelled to Messina. The Messina police force soon reported that Bodoki had boarded a vessel called *La Bella Galatea* in the company of a certain Tiberio Vida—a fellow Hungarian and presumed accomplice—and sailed for Naples.

The Naples police confirmed that Bodoki and Vida had spent time together there too, and indeed Signore Vida seemed to have brought Bodoki almost as far as Rome. It was impossible that this Vida could merely be some travelling tourist, since he had spent just a single morning amid the delights of Naples, before hurrying on. No, this Vida was beyond question another suspicious character. Suspicions were further increased by the discovery that, before leaving Palermo, Vida had told the hotel that he would return after a few days' tour round the south and west of the island. Instead, however, he had driven straight for Messina that very night. He had to be a fugitive on the run from the law.

All this was known by the fifteenth of March, and on the afternoon of the same day, an urgent telegram was sent to all municipal police departments ordering them to stop anyone driving a dark blue Lancia of the newer model and ask for their papers. If they found either Tiberio Vida or Andrea Bodoki they were to arrest them immediately, along with anyone who happened to be travelling with them.

The head of the Padua police department was a man by the name of Boccatorsa. He had been in the force for almost twenty-five years now, but his career had been a frustrating succession of dead-ends and missed opportunities. His own long-held belief was that his misfortunate surname (which means something like 'twisted mouth' in Italian) was responsible for his bad luck. He had always hated the name, having been chased, teased and bullied at school because of it. There were few police chiefs in Italy more eager than Boccatorsa to prove their worth, and few more diligent in the performance of their duties.

During the government of Luigi Facta he had not only zealously hunted fascists but had even conspired with the left-wing Italian Radical Party, since he believed their leader, Francesco Nitti, the most likely figure to next win power. This was all the more congenial to him since he and Nitti were both natives of Naples. Events, however, took quite a different turn and Mussolini's march on Rome scuppered all his carefully laid plans.

Immediately after Mussolini's seizure of power he had, naturally, switched sides, but with little success. He soon found himself transferred from the sun-drenched seafronts of Bari to this dreary northern city on the endless plains of the Po river valley. Bari, what is more, had almost a hundred and twenty thousand inhabitants at the time, while little Padua was a city of barely fifty thousand. This setback had been a heavy blow to Boccatorsa, especially as he considered himself a man of great and unappreciated talent. He burned for some great crime to uncover, so that all those who had passed him over for promotion might at last see what a capable man they had overlooked! Down in Bari, the largest port in the south-east of Italy, he might have hoped for some such case, but here? What had ever happened in Padua? Even the tourists just stopped off to see the cathedral baptistery, the Scrovegni Chapel and a church or two, before heading back to Verona or Venice.

It seemed hopeless, or at least it did until around lunchtime on the sixteenth of May, when Tibor Vida unexpectedly turned up outside the police station. When the latest documents of the Bodoki case arrived by airmail later that same afternoon, his prospects seemed even brighter. Fortune, at long last, had shone on Boccatorsa! Here, finally, was a criminal case of national—even international—importance. Now they would see the sort of policeman he was!

Examining the two seized passports, what caught his eye at once was that the woman worked for Hungary's largest newspaper. That was why he interviewed her first: he was determined that this should be an international story. When Mrs Anderson asked whether she might be permitted to telegraph her newspaper's Rome correspondent, therefore, he was almost indecently eager to oblige, especially as he hoped that by keeping the press 'sweet' they might be more likely to write favourably about him. A long-distance call was placed to Rome and he himself also spoke to the correspondent, who of course confirmed Mrs Anderson's identity.

While they were waiting for the call to be connected, Boccatorsa decided to ask a few questions.

Mrs Anderson told the truth, explaining that she had first met Tibor Vida in Palermo. She naturally spoke highly of him, but being convinced that they had been arrested on her account through information obtained from Lakatos, she gave the impression that Vida was a rather superficial acquaintance; she wanted to involve him as little as possible. She had travelled north with him, she said, because he was driving back to Hungary himself and it seemed easier than taking the train. When Boccatorsa asked about Bodoki she said she had never seen the man before he appeared in Messina, and never saw him again after they parted ways in Genzano. She confided that she had always seen him as a slightly shady character, but knew nothing for sure.

She told only the truth, but not the whole truth. She said nothing about the painting, for instance, and nothing about Lakatos. Instead, she simply answered the questions that were put to her, and though she chose her words carefully it did not show in her manner. Nor did anything betray her suspicion that she—through her acquaintance with Lakatos—was responsible for their arrest.

Vida, as the reader will have guessed, made a decidedly bad impression during his first interview, but quite the opposite was true of Mrs Anderson. She was attractive and composed, and her big brown eyes always looked straight at Boccatorsa with an expression of frank good nature. Italians, after all—even Italians as severe as Boccatorsa—are so easily moved by beauty, and she was undeniably a beautiful woman. He did not even really interrogate her closely, and his questions were more for form's sake. Walking her to the door, he told her that it would be impossible to have her released that same evening, but that he would write his report tomorrow and recommend her immediate discharge. It would still take a few days to sort everything out, but from the next day he expected she would be able to stay in a hotel until her formal release papers came though.

It happened just as he said, and Mrs Anderson spent the next evening in the Croce d'Oro hotel. They did not even post a guard.

This was a relief. At first she had been worried that her release was just a trick to see if she would meet some anti-fascist collaborator. To test this theory she called her colleague in Rome, telling him that she had been released and thanking him for his help. The call only lasted three minutes and the only real reason she made it was to listen for the slight echo which always indicated that someone else was listening in. The sound was perfectly clear: nobody had monitored her call.

She took a walk down to the cathedral and had a look round the shops, all to see if someone was following her. No, she was certain that there was nobody. This was an even bigger relief.

When she got back to the hotel she hoped that Tibor might already be there waiting for her, but there was no sign of him.

When would he be released? Why hang on to him if they had already let her go? There was only one possible reason; that stupid alteration to the registration plates! That was the only possible crime they could be interested in, since Tibor had not the slightest connection to the Lakatos affair, and she could think of no other grounds for detaining him.

Might they wait until afternoon before releasing him? Or perhaps evening?

She waited. Sitting alone in her hotel room, her anxiety grew steadily more acute. That night she hardly slept.

At dawn she decided that something had to be done. At eight she called her colleague in Rome, to be sure of catching him at home. He was a good-natured, helpful gentleman of late middle-age, and very knowledgeable in the workings of the Italian bureaucracy. She knew him well from another story they had once worked on together. She explained that Tibor Vida was a famous opera composer who had been arrested for changing his car registration plates. There was an incredulous snort from the other end of the line.

'He did what? Why would he do a daft thing like that?'

'There was another car on the same stretch of road that was looking for us. They knew our registration number too. We were trying to avoid getting caught by them…' Telling him how they changed the numbers in Florence, she gave the impression that it had been all or partly her idea, so as to lessen her partner's responsibility.

The older man laughed.

'Can it be that the redoubtable Milla Anderson has finally had her head turned by a man? Well, congratulations. I know Tibor Vida; he's a relatively serious sort of fellow and a gentleman. You could certainly have done worse…'

'Please,' she said, interrupting. 'Promise me: you never heard a word of this.'

'All right, all right, I promise. This stays strictly between us. But tell me, how can I be of service?'

'In just one thing. I want you to go straight to the Hungarian Embassy and tell them what has happened. The Embassy will surely step in to represent the cause of such a distinguished citizen; after all, his operas have won Hungary renown abroad and success at home, and the whole thing with the number plates is surely only a misdemeanour at most.'

'You're quite right. He'll pay a fine—no great matter for a man of his means—then waltz straight through the prison gates. I'll head over to the Embassy before lunchtime and talk to them. Anyhow, I'm sorry Milla but I really must dash. Ciao! And good luck!'

That was good. It was even better when he called back at lunchtime to say that the Embassy had agreed to begin working for Tibor's release that same day.

She waited impatiently, hoping that they might be reunited that same evening.

It was already getting dark when a maid knocked on the door to say that a gentleman was asking for her. Her heart soared; he had been released at last!

'Of course! Send him up at once!'

The man who walked into the room, however, was not Tibor Vida but Schönberg-Belmonte.

'*Na, meine Gnädige*,' he said in German. 'My dear lady! At last we meet again!'

He spoke these words after sitting down uninvited in the only armchair and so stretching out his great bulk that he seemed to fill half the room. He gave a jovial laugh.

'No thanks to you, I might add; you certainly gave us a chase! You wanted to get away from me, but that's not quite so easy as it looks, is it? If good old Uncle Schönberg has you in his sights, you can bet you won't slip out of them again. Better by far to come clean now.'

'What do you want?' Milla asked coldly.

'I came, my dear, to continue the delightful conversation we had in Palermo.'

She did not reply, so he went on.

'This is our last chance to come to some sort of arrangement, and I have decided that the offer I made in Palermo still stands. Indeed, I am willing to go further if you name a specific price, but I won't be drawn into giving speculative offers. Tell me, what are you asking for it?'

'I don't have it. Our cases were impounded when we were arrested and I still haven't got that one back.'

'I know. I know everything. I know you saw through that little idiot Bodoki too, and grilled him pretty hard over his bungling. No less than I'd do myself! I know there's an arrest warrant for Bodoki too, but I've made sure he's well hidden. One minute he's there, the next he's gone. Nobody's going to find him now...' An evil twinkle shone for a moment in those tiny eyes, then he shrugged and went on. 'But that's all by the by. The main thing now is for each of us to set out clearly where we stand. So tell me, *Liebchen*, how much do you want?'

Milla did not reply. A voice inside her head kept telling her that she was utterly alone. She had nobody to turn to, nobody she could lean on for protection, and was completely at the mercy of a man capable of... Well, who knew? And what had he meant about young Bodoki?

Schönberg seemed able to read her thoughts.

'You are alone now, my dear. Entirely alone. I can do with you, so to speak, as I please. Don't you worry your little head about that, though; old Uncle Schöni won't let you come to any harm. You know why? Because you don't have anything worth taking. What are you? A penniless little journalist girl? What kind of a life is that, slaving away for small change? Is that what you want? Or maybe you think this knight in shining armour, this Tibor Vida, is going to whisk you away and marry you? Don't make me laugh! The man's an opera composer! A man like that has had a hundred women in his bed, and he'll have a hundred more after you. How do you think all those pretty little opera divas and chorus singers get on in the world? Men like that never marry, you can take my word for it.'

There was another pause as Schönberg adjusted his arm in the sling, then he looked up again.

'I'm going to be entirely honest with you. The truth is that you're a very clever, very capable young woman. I know how to weigh up my opponents, as well as my own side, since I am a clever and capable man myself. You, however, are capable in a way that is exceedingly rare to find, and you have got taste too. I've got an eye for that sort of thing. So listen here, I'm going to make you an offer. Not only will I give you all the money I promised last time, but I'll even let you in on the business. Only after you've given me the painting, of course… You have to understand, though; a business like mine means real money. Big money. A fortune, in fact. I already make more than I know what to do with, but with the two of us working together…' He lapsed into silence for a moment, his face like that of a greedy child picturing some promised cornucopia. 'With your looks, your charm, and your brains, combined with my knowledge of the world… The two of us could accomplish things others couldn't even imagine!'

A shudder of disgust ran through Milla's body, and she stammered a little as she spoke.

'What do—me and you? How—how can you even imagine…?'

'How can I imagine it? Easiest thing in the world, my dear! You and I would both live in Paris. Oh, don't worry, I'm not suggesting anything *carnal* between us; I don't need you like that! But we'd share a little mansion where we would entertain high-society guests, finding out which treasures are stashed in which stately homes. Then it's just a matter of taking a trip out there in person, scoping out the possibilities; nothing very taxing for a woman of your talents…' Lowering his voice, he spoke in a purr of self-admiration. 'The rest can be left to me.'

Milla raised a hand as though to ward off this dreadful vision, but Schönberg went on.

'Take your time. I'm not expecting an answer straight away, but think clearly about your situation. There are two possibilities. Either you hand over the painting or you don't. If you hand it over then you're back where you were before, scraping a living in an expensive city like Budapest. Also, no matter how cleverly we arrange the hand-over—you leave it locked in your hotel room, perhaps, and I steal it from there—there is always going to be a trace of suspicion hanging over you, and rumours that you might have somehow been involved. That's unavoidable, especially if they discover you have a secret stash of dollars. Why would you choose that, a life of hardship and penury, constantly trying to hide the money you made, when I'm offering you the perfect escape?'

166

She looked at him in silence for a moment, then spoke quietly.

'And if I don't hand it over?'

'If you don't hand it over…' Schönberg's heavy, ponderous body seemed to swell at once with titanic strength, dwarfing the armchair he sat in. 'If you don't hand it over then I will break you into a thousand tiny pieces. Understand, woman, that there is nothing I wouldn't do! Nothing!' He paused, speaking his next words with exaggerated emphasis. 'You had better be careful. Bodoki just vanished, remember, and there's nothing to stop the same thing happening to you.'

She felt cold fear at her throat and in the pit of her stomach. She was alone here. Defenceless. It would be easy to break into this room in the middle of the night, or to grab her in the corridor. There were a thousand possibilities for men as brutal and unscrupulous as Schönberg. Perhaps his thugs were already standing outside the door, ready at a single word of command to burst in and seize her, bundling her off into the night… She had to play for time until Tibor was finally freed, or until she could persuade her colleague in Rome to come here and help her. But she had to think fast to escape the danger she was presently in.

'All right,' she said slowly. 'I'll hand it over, just as soon as it's back in my possession and I can do it safely.'

She was careful to add this precondition; even now she wanted to leave herself as much room for manoeuvre as possible.

'You see? I knew you were a clever girl. So we have a deal?'

'Yes—but not straight away. After all, I don't even have it at the moment. Later, though, when I get it back, I promise. We'll need to wait for the right opportunity, though, and you'll have to do it through me.'

Schönberg reverted at once to his jovial, good-natured persona.

'Of course, of course! An old man like me knows these things take time. I can wait. Not forever, mind you, but I can wait. And I'll always be somewhere close by. You might not always see me, but I'll be around. In any case, let's shake on it, then I'll be on my way.'

He stretched out an enormous palm and Milla met it with her slender hand, not without a tremor of loathing as those strong, fleshy fingers closed on it. The thought flashed through her mind that those same fingers on her throat could easily choke the life out of her.

Walking towards the door, Schönberg stopped and turned back, his voice again full of menace.

'I just want to say one more thing. If it ever comes into your pretty little head to go to the police then I'll hear about it at once. If that happens…' He drew one finger across his throat, then walked out of the room and closed the door.

Milla stood motionless for a few moments, her pulse hammering in her temples, then hurried over to the door. Her room was at the end of the corridor, and with her eye to the peephole she could make out three men walking towards the stairs. One was Schönberg, while the other two were big, broad-shouldered men. So there really had been thugs outside! Heaven only knew what would have happened if she had given a different answer!

She went over to the window, opened it and looked out. A big touring car was parked outside the hotel. Not the tulip-red one that had followed them on the road to Padua, but an apple-green one of a similar size and build. Night had already fallen, but two electric lights by the main hotel entrance meant she could see it clearly enough. She watched as the three men walked out of the hotel, got into the car and drove off.

What now? What now? What now? Oh, if only Tibor were free! Then they could have driven off into the night again. A day on the road would be enough to reach the Hungarian border, where at last they would be safe!

Well, perhaps tomorrow he would be released. The thought comforted her a little.

VIII

Vida remained in prison.

The Hungarian Embassy took up his case in Rome, but the Italian Home Office explained that the altered number plate was really a quite incidental matter, and of no importance except as it related to a different and altogether graver crime of which he was the prime suspect. There was no possibility of releasing him as a favour, at least until the facts of the case became clearer.

This information was not supplied directly from the Home Office to the Hungarian Embassy, but through the Foreign Office, the only ministry with whom embassies are officially allowed to liaise. This was to remain the case, and the constant back and forth between various departments and ministries would significantly slow the pace of inquiries. Memos were sent here and there, and telephone calls forwarded through a branching maze of switchboards. At last the Home Office requested copies of all documents relevant to the case, and on the third day the Hungarian *chargé d'affaires* was able to examine the long list of suspicions which Boccatorsa had compiled about Vida, along with embellished descriptions of his aggressive behaviour in custody. The man was, according to these notes, a wild and dangerous criminal, very probably the leader of the gang which had stolen the Leonardo from the Budapest Museum. The *chargé d'affaires* happened to know Vida personally and considered these allegations an absolute impossibility. To disprove them, however, he needed a written character statement on Vida from the Hungarian police, and this could only be obtained by sending an encrypted telegram to Budapest. Encryption was a fiddly, time-consuming business, both in composing the message and in decrypting it at the other end, and this was of course equally true of the reply. Another day passed.

Luckily, however, the Embassy passed on everything it learned of the case to Milla's colleague in Rome, who in turn phoned her to relay the current state of affairs. Knowing this, she was at last able to act. She immediately telephoned her editor in Budapest and told him everything that had happened to herself and Vida over the previous few weeks.

Time passed for Milla at an almost unbearable crawl; all she could do was wait, and wait, and wait, knowing nothing of how events were unfolding around her. The news from Rome helped to an extent, since it proved she had not been the direct cause of their arrest and so alleviated some of the guilt and self-reproach she had lived with over the past few days. In another sense, of course, it simply made things worse: Vida could remain in prison for years! He would never have ended up in this awful mess if he had not met her, and if she had not manipulated him into buying that picture. It was all her fault, she told herself, and she cursed her own stupidity.

On several occasions she considered returning to the police headquarters and begging them for help, but she knew Schönberg was watching—even to set foot in that place was to court danger. Besides, it almost certainly wouldn't do any good. The only tool at her disposal was the telephone, and she used it almost ceaselessly in an effort to help coordinate the work of the Hungarian police and the Embassy in Rome, as well as the newspaper offices in Budapest. At last their combined efforts bore fruit: Boccatorsa received orders from Rome to release Vida at once. Not only that, but he was also officially reprimanded: how could he have been so blind as not to see that he was dealing with a distinguished foreign national? All his carefully listed suspicions were now used against him; his superiors accused him of 'relying more on idle fancy and conjecture than evidence and police work', and he was even threatened with dismissal if he continued to cause headaches for Rome. He was further ordered to make a personal apology to Vida.

Poor Boccatorsa was beside himself. He made a grudging apology to Vida and set him free with all his possessions, including the trunk with the picture at the bottom. The reader may raise an eyebrow at the idea of an Italian police chief simply handing back a stolen Leonardo da Vinci, but in truth it never crossed his mind. Boccatorsa's only wish was to be rid of everything connected to that accursed case. He now exits our story, and we shall hear no more of him— all the less since he suffered an acute nervous breakdown shortly after Vida's departure and took to his bed. When, next day, he received an urgent message ordering him to send the painting to the Hungarian Embassy in Rome so it could be transported securely to Budapest, he had to reply that the composer had left the day before with everything he owned, and so he was unable to comply with this order.

Milla, when she got the news from Rome that Tibor was to be released the next day, felt a sudden rush of joy. Anxiety too, though, since his release meant that the most dangerous part of their journey would soon be upon them. They had to try to escape Schönberg again, and make a dash for Hungary. Schönberg, however, was sure to be watching closely, and would attempt any murderous gambit to stop them.

These were the thoughts preoccupying her on that last night, when she knew that Tibor would be released the next morning, the twenty-second of March. She telephoned Rome and, through her colleague, asked the Embassy if they would take responsibility for the picture. She did not want it to be with her and Tibor on this perilous stretch of their journey. She received no reply that evening, however, nor by noon the next day.

Time passed, and she spent all that next morning preparing herself mentally for the dangers to come. There were also difficult decisions to be made. Should she stay here until evening, or perhaps even until the next day, waiting for someone to come and take the picture away? No! That was impossible! Staying here was much too risky; Schönberg's men could easily break into her room during the night. Anything, indeed, was better than staying here, where Schönberg knew *her* whereabouts precisely and she knew nothing of *his*. She had to do something, though, and try to prepare for any of the countless eventualities which might arise.

She spent long, restless hours lying in bed and staring up into the darkness, thinking. The bells of the cathedral were tolling Mass when she left the Croce d'Oro the next morning. Walking a little way down Via Dante she soon came to the shop of Egisto Ristorini. This was a strange and remarkable little place with '*Tagliatore e Intarsiatore*'— woodcarver and inlayer—on the sign hanging above the door. In the shop window was an almost life-sized portrait of King Victor Emmanuel II, which had been made entirely of different kinds of wood. The brow was of white maple; his hair, enormous moustache and long goatee beard of dark rosewood. The whites of his eyes were ivory, the irises ebony, while little sections of orangewood added a touch of colour to his cheeks. Above it all were the words '*il re galant'uomo*'— the cavalier king—in an elegant, swirling script. It was a very striking piece of work, and truly an excellent likeness of that pugnacious—if also rather pug-faced—monarch. There was always something slightly incongruous about the vast quantities of facial hair framing those snubbed, babyish features. In any case, Signore Ristorini had evidently put many hours into the composition and execution of this masterpiece, made to celebrate the fiftieth anniversary of the Battle of Königgrätz, which liberated Padua from Austrian suzerainty and made it part of the Kingdom of Italy. The celebrations, alas, never took place, since by that date—1916—Italy was in a life-or-death struggle with the Austro-Hungarian Empire. This magnificent piece of work therefore remained unused by the municipality, and served now only to advertise the skill of its maker. It stood in the shop window alongside smaller but no less painstakingly crafted portraits in wood. There were women and men, children and the elderly, presumably representing the entire extended family of Signore Ristorini. All had been done in the same fashion as the king, with different shades of wood used to highlight different features, and all were lacquered to a shine. Signs advertised the craftsman's ability to capture any likeness in inlaid wood, even from a photograph.

Whether these advertisements were successful or not was another matter, however, and we may suppose that business was in fact rather slow. This should hardly come as a surprise: however much skill and effort are expended in their creation, such handicrafts rarely manage to overcome an inherent and inescapable tastelessness. Indeed, with their alarmingly accented eyes and rouged cheeks, these inlaid portraits were of a species of kitsch which one really only finds in Italy, this supposed citadel of refinement and good taste. Visitors wandering the streets of any popular Italian city invariably find themselves besieged by hawkers of seashells painted with images of Vesuvius, mosaics of Venetian gondolas, matchboxes covered in tiny snail shells, tortoiseshell toothpicks and the like. Who buys these things? There doesn't appear to be anyone—aside perhaps from a few *petit-bourgeois* Germans— who actually *likes* them, but that does not appear to dissuade us from buying them as gifts for others.

Signore Ristorini, in any case, would not have recognised this description of his artistic output, and had anyone dared tell him that it lacked taste he would have dismissed the charge as rank philistinism. He took great pride in his craft, and if business was bad then he consoled himself with the thought that Michelangelo too often went unrecognised by his contemporaries.

Signore Ristorini happened to be standing outside his shop when Milla reached that part of the street. As befits a hardworking craftsman, he was a rather pudgy man with a prominent pot belly peeping out from beneath his shirt, and his bald pate was concealed beneath a red fez with a long blue tassel hanging down behind his ear. He was, in accordance with long-established habit, standing with his hands in his pockets and patiently awaiting the forever-delayed arrival of eager shoppers. It came as a great surprise—almost a miracle—when he glanced up again and realised that the elegantly dressed young woman he had seen strolling down the street was making straight for him! For his shop!

'*Prego, signorina, entrate, entrate!*' he babbled, bowing low. The silk tassel of his fez capered excitedly behind his ear, equally animated by the arrival of this unexpected visitor.

He began by showing her all his finest wares, including Sant'Antonio in a range of different sizes, all made from ivory, tortoiseshell and ebony. The Archangel Michael had been given hair of bamboo root and a halo of yellow lemonwood, while a varnished mahogany Satan snarled and writhed as he was trampled beneath the angelic feet. There were several Madonnas too, most taking after either Raphael or Guido Reni, with mother-of-pearl faces and strips of polished brass suggesting radiant light. Signore Ristorini, however, did not press these religious images upon his visitor with much conviction; instead, he urged her to let him capture her own beautiful features in wood. With just a photograph he could create a portrait of her that would outshine anything presently on display.

'*Un ritratto, signorina!*'—A portrait!

He showed her various finished specimens, alongside photographs to demonstrate how well he had captured their likenesses in wood. The blue silk tassel danced jubilantly back and forth as the plump little *maestro* rushed around, pulling this or that old piece down from the shelves.

But nothing quite matched what Milla was looking for. Commissioning a portrait was out of the question; she had no time for that, and though she praised the many religious works, they were all much too small. She needed something bigger; something around forty-five by thirty-five centimetres… Yes, that was what she needed, she told Signore Ristorini, and that was the only thing she had any interest in buying.

There was nothing like that here, though; everything was much too small.

The blue silk tassel sank dejectedly behind Signore Ristorini's ear, then abruptly bounced aloft with new hope.

There *was* something after all! Perhaps he had just the thing!

Hurrying over to the window, he lifted down the life-sized profile of Victor Emmanuel.

'This, perhaps? Is this the sort of thing you are looking for?' His voice was now tinged with anxiety; he had nothing else remotely this large.

'Let's measure it,' she said.

It came to forty-five by thirty-two.

'How much?' she asked.

'Oh, *signorina*, this is a very valuable piece. *Preziosissimo!* This is our great king, *il Re Liberatore!'*

He went on to explain what a perfect likeness it was of the illustrious man, and how many hours had gone into its execution. This was his masterpiece, the unsurpassed and perhaps unsurpassable pinnacle of his career, and he doubted whether a finer inlaid wood portrait existed in all the world. He made broad, sweeping gestures as he spoke, the silk tassel bouncing up and down as though in earnest agreement with every assertion. None of this made much impression on Milla, however, and when she spoke her voice was coldly objective.

'Well? Is it for sale or isn't it?'

Ristorini quickly quoted a price—three hundred lire—lest his visitor should lose patience and leave. Milla bargained him down to a hundred and sixty. That was all right, she would pay that much. Still, something troubled her about the picture. It was the right height and breadth, but not nearly thick enough. She turned back to Ristorini.

'Could you perhaps sell me two walnut boards of the same size as the portrait? I'd like to have a case made for it.'

Well, that was no trouble at all; Ristorini was delighted to be of service, since for more than a decade he had found nobody remotely interested in buying his Victor Emmanuel. He disappeared into his workshop and soon re-emerged with two boards that fit the wooden portrait to within a centimetre. These only added a few lire to the total. Ristorini wrapped the package in paper and tied it up with string, then Milla paid and he accompanied her out into the street. He bowed low to her as she departed, the blue tassel of his fez bobbing with equally sincere gratitude. For a long time afterward it could not keep still, but twitched about as though yearning to follow in the footsteps of that spellbinding woman. Alas, the thin cord held it in bondage, and at length it sank resignedly to its habitual spot behind Signore Ristorini's ear.

Milla went into two other shops on her way back to the hotel. In one she bought silk paper and ribbon, in the other a mass of cotton wadding. The cathedral bells were just tolling noon as she climbed the steps to the hotel entrance.

Barely an hour later the little blue Lancia pulled up in front of the Croce d'Oro, and out leapt Tibor Vida. Taking the stairs four at a time he bounded up to the first floor and along the corridor, where Milla met him in a wild embrace. They kissed, hugged, laughed and cried, then kissed again and babbled over one another in their anxiety to know the other was all right. Tibor told her about Boccatorsa's rage— and his sulky apology—and his wild feeling of liberation as he got behind the wheel of his car once again. They talked for a long time, interrupting one another with laughs, jokes and urgent questions. Then Milla's face grew fractionally more serious, and she told him about Schönberg's visit. She left many things out, downplaying her own fear and the presence of the two thugs outside. She did not want to alarm her lover unnecessarily, or to upset his joyful mood. All she said was that she had been forced to make a dishonest promise to him, but of course mentioned nothing about Schönberg's offer of a shared life in Paris and all the rest of it. What would have been the point? After all, there was no question of her giving up the painting without a fight. Not at any price.

They set about packing her things, then carried everything down to the car.

Then they were off. Away! They roared out of Padua like two birds freed from a cage, heading for Treviso and Udine.

Then onward to Austria!

Only one *autostrada* leads north towards the border, and while there were other, more circuitous routes, Milla judged it useless at this point to try to throw Schönberg off their trail. In any case, he would surely still trust her to find some way of fulfilling her end of the bargain. Only when they got close to the border, and Schönberg began to suspect she had misled him, would danger threaten.

That, however, was simply a danger that had to be faced. It was unavoidable. Sooner or later, she knew, she and her enemy would once more come face to face.

So they drove on, their happiness tempered by a—well-founded—touch of fear.

From the Diary of Tibor Vida

Klagenfurt, Austria, 23rd of March, afternoon
We were almost at the end of that last, splendid drive through Italy. So fine was the country along the banks of the Isonzo, in fact, that the thought of the hunters pursuing us often slipped my mind entirely. Our route ran between steep mountains which form the westernmost extreme of that great Karst Plateau which stretches deep into the Slovene-speaking regions of northern Yugoslavia. Still, while 'Karst' evokes images of bare, fissured limestone, the country we drove through seemed positively bursting with life. Green forests—presumably planted and tended by the Austrians before this region was ceded to Italy after the war—rose on either hand, snow-capped mountains glinting in the sunlight beyond. Cliffs and jagged pillars of rock filled the middle distance, and whatever a crag does when it beetles, they were doing a cracking job of it amid those eagle-haunted summits. Every now and then a bend in the road would afford a glimpse of some great white glacier, before another turn concealed it again. The river swirled along the valley

floor beneath us, its meltwaters cobalt blue and as opaque as fresh Hungarian sour cream. I think it's the half-melted slush that gives it this thick, creamy appearance, as well as the limestone dust that gets swept down off the mountains by the melting snow. Our road was a few hundred metres up the hillside from the river, and we sped parallel to its coursing current like a pair of hawks on outspread wings.

My little Lancia tore along with fresh, eager energy. She has no silencer to speak of, and the four-stroke engine hammered a joyous, deafening rhythm. The road inclined upwards, shadowing the course of the river, but my little car's pace never slowed, and the speedometer remained continually above fifty. Sometimes I glanced in the rear-view mirror, where I was often able to see for miles back down the valley we had climbed. Far off in the distance I could just make out the big, dark-coloured car following us. Had we been on the flat they would surely have gradually closed on us as before, but on rising ground my lighter vehicle had the advantage, and the distance between us steadily increased. If Schönberg's great bulk was weighing them down too, then I had no doubt that we would be over the Predil Pass and into Austria before they had a chance to catch us. I can hardly describe the thrill of it.

The Predil Pass, noon
There's a splendid little lake of purest, crystal blue, ringed all about by pines. The shallow water by the lakeshore is the

same cobalt blue as the Isonzo, but soon shelves off, through ever-deeper shades, until it's almost black. These alpine lakes are all unimaginably deep. The craggy cliffs surrounding it are also coal-black, and I could already feel the shift from sun-drenched Italy to the northern, Germanic world.

There was a little restaurant by the shores of the lake, and after clearing my exit papers with the Italian customs officials I asked them to look after my car while Milolu and I went for some lunch. It would, I decided, probably be as safe there as anywhere.

We sat on an open terrace overlooking the mirrored surface of the lake. There was a chill in the air on account of the altitude, but the fresh whiff of mountain ozone was so invigorating that we barely noticed the cold. The waitress came over and we both ordered trout from the lake below. They were served quickly, still covered in pitch-black scales. Trout change colour as they grow to match the dominant colour of their surroundings, and the only highlights remaining were in the small red spots that still speckled their flanks. My word, they were delicious! I don't think I've ever eaten such fine trout in all my life! Firm, juicy flesh that peeled away in succulent mouthfuls, and hardly a bone!

We were just setting about these tremendous fish when a big black touring car pulled into the restaurant car park and the doors opened. It was not Schönberg and his gang who stepped from it, but two men and two women whom I had never seen before. They paid no attention whatsoever to us, but sat down at a nearby table and ordered the same trout dish we had, then began joking and laughing among themselves.

Well, this just put the cherry on top of my rising good spirits. Might we have given them the slip after all?

When I bought the car I also got a sort of international customs pass to stick on the windscreen. It's a fine invention; the border guard writes down the number on the front, and within a few minutes you're free to cross from one country to another. We had no trouble from the Austrian customs officials; in fact they were very polite. Leaving the checkpoint behind, we sped down pine-clad hillsides and were in Villach within an hour.

I had hoped that the drive from there to Klagenfurt would be equally straightforward, but was disappointed; something went wrong with the spark plugs and the engine began misfiring. I opened the bonnet and had a look. One plug had definitely blown, and I changed it, but when we set off again I sensed at once that the engine still wasn't right. It seemed increasingly likely that the problem lay in the carburettor; a thing of mystery far beyond my rudimentary mechanical skill. We stopped again and I cleaned the fuel-injector nozzle, but that didn't seem to do much good.

We were a long way behind schedule by the time we got close to Klagenfurt, and my car limped and rattled along the shores of the Wörthersee. At last though, long after dark, we made it into town. I've just now got the car checked into the hotel garage and I'll look it over properly tomorrow.

24th of March, morning

I made sure the car was parked somewhere secure while Milolu kept an eye on the bags. When I got back I found her sitting in our shared room. She had not unpacked anything, and was just sitting by the desk staring blankly at the wall. An opened letter was sitting on the desk in front of her, and she handed it to me without a word.

There were only two typewritten words: '*Wann? Wo?*'— When? Where? I didn't understand at first, and frowned at her in puzzlement. She replied with a single word, spoken very softly:

'Schönberg.'

The chambermaid had given it to her, saying it had arrived before us that afternoon. Milolu now confessed to me that she had received a note with the same two words at the hotel in Udine where we stayed last night. There too the porter said it had arrived before us.

That old gangster isn't hot on our trail, he's three steps ahead of us! I have the queasy feeling that he's all around us, invisible yet omnipresent.

I don't mind admitting that it's starting to prey on my nerves.

What the devil are we to do? Go to the police? Ask for a bodyguard and an escort to the Hungarian border? But what could we say? We don't even know for sure that Schönberg's in the country, or how he got here if he is. Nor have we any idea what alias or aliases he might be operating under; I'm sure for a man like him it's very little trouble to supply himself with a new passport and nationality. The Austrians would think we were mad—they'd probably laugh us out of the station! I've developed, I think, a more realistic appraisal of my powers of persuasion—and the inherent power of the truth to overcome all doubts—after those absurd interviews with Boccatorsa. No, I'm not going through all that again!

All we can do is keep our wits about us and try to slip through the net. Nothing else for it.

We haven't left our hotel room since I got back, and even had dinner sent up. Both of us have tried to keep up a front of careless high spirits but I know she's faking it, and she surely knows the same about me. Before going to bed last night we decided to barricade the door. I dragged the big chest of drawers across it, then stacked the water bottle and glasses on top; they would have made an almighty racket if anyone had tried to force the door.

Crawling into bed, we curled up close to one another like two children alone at night in a rustling forest, watched by numberless pairs of unseen eyes. Every faint noise made us start, every footfall in the corridor outside made the hair rise on the backs of our necks. Was that the creak of a door? Did a car stop outside our hotel? Were those footsteps on the stairs? Did the latch just click? No, it was just the hot water pipes—or was it? Neither of us got any real sleep, just a few fitful, restless dozes. Mostly we lay in silence, staring wide-eyed into the inky blackness.

Dawn broke at last, and poor Milolu was at last able to get an hour or two of sleep. She slept deeply, lines of infinite fatigue etched across her features. I lay watching her, feeling the apparitions of the night fade as daylight filled the room.

The hotel gradually came to life, and I heard the tinkling of bottles as the milkman dropped off a crate by the entrance. Then there was the sound of the front door being unlocked and the rhythmic swish of someone sweeping the pavement outside… For me too there was blessed relief—almost redemption—in the new day.

The same day, noon
Well, we're still stuck in Klagenfurt. The car is in a better state than it was but still not good enough to risk a long journey on the open road. I've just spent the whole morning taking it apart and putting it back together in the garage; it's an ungodly amount of work. First thing was the oil; it's something I meant to deal with back in Palermo, and we've driven well over a thousand kilometres since then. I drained the alarmingly opaque sludge from the bottom of the tank and replaced it with fresh stuff from the bottle, then greased the wheel bearings. I also filtered the petrol twice to make sure no grit clogs the engine, and ran a fairly systematic electrical test, isolating each component to check that it was

in working order. I thought we were ready, but when I turned the key in the ignition it soon became clear that there was a problem with the dynamo. At that point I gave up. Taking the car round to a local mechanic, I asked him to have a look for me; he said it should be ready to go within two hours or so.

It's costing us time, of course, but I'd rather endure delays here than find ourselves stranded on that long stretch of deserted road running from here to the Yugoslav border. Imagine getting stuck there at night… No, any delay here is preferable to that!

While tinkering with the car I kept obsessively calculating time and distance. Even if we set off by mid-afternoon we'd be unlikely to get further than the Yugoslav city of Marburg, and that's still a long way short of the Hungarian frontier. That means another night abroad, and if the Austrian frontier posed no impediment to our pursuers then there's no reason to suppose Yugoslavia will be any different; we could well be in for another bad night's sleep. That's when it occurred to me that I happen to have an old friend in Marburg, a chap I used to go drinking with during my student days at the Music Academy in Vienna. He was a friendly, happy-go-lucky sort of fellow with a flair for fashion, and everybody liked him. He gave up music in the end and retrained as a lawyer, and of course like everyone else of our generation he was called up during the war; I bumped into him once or twice on the Bosnian front. We haven't been much in contact since then, but he wrote to me last year to congratulate me on the success of *Shakuntala*. He also wrote that he had been elected to the city council and that things were going well for him. He's Slovenian, and while back in Vienna I always knew him as Carl Ruditsch, it seems that these days he goes by the name of Dragutin Rudić, just as his city, which comes more naturally to me by the old Austrian name of Marburg, is known to the Yugoslavs as Maribor.

In any case, it occurred to me that we might be better off staying with him than in some unfamiliar hotel; a private house is always so much more secure. We could even explain, in person, our reasons for imposing upon him at such short notice. I called his number on the long-distance phone, and was in luck; he answered at once, and willingly accepted my proposed visit. Indeed, he sounded delighted at the prospect.

After that I walked back to the hotel. Entering the room, I asked Milolu if anyone had tried the door or sought to contact her. No, she said, there had not been a soul all morning. The only thing—well—about an hour and a half before, it had seemed as though the spherical door-handle had twisted to the right... But she could not be sure, she said, and had probably simply imagined it. She had listened closely, but heard no footsteps in the corridor outside.

Three in the afternoon
The Lancia is here at last, and seems in perfect condition. We

hurriedly brought the luggage down, as much as we could carry at once, and slung it into the boot in no particular order. I fastened the strap that keeps the heavier things from sliding about on the road, and then we were off.

It's a hundred and forty kilometres from here to Marburg, and about two thirds of the way there we cross the Yugoslav frontier. I hope we can make it.

IX

Zalaegerszeg, Hungary, 25th of March, evening

So much has happened to me over the past twenty-four hours or so that I'm not even sure I can get it straight enough in my head to write down. Never, not even in the war, have I gone through anything like what happened yesterday afternoon. I should take a deep breath and consciously put events in their correct order, or else I'll just get confused and muddle it all up.

The weather was closing in by the time we left Klagenfurt; clouds came down over the Alps like a grey quilt and hid the mountaintops from view. Wisps of fog began to trail through the roadside pines, and before long a thin rain was falling. It was cold and damp—real flu weather—and having come straight from the balmy climes of Italy, it was a bit of a shock. I don't feel the cold too badly but Milolu looked half-frozen, and I asked her why she didn't get the blanket from the back.

She looked back to where the blanket lay over our things on the back seat. All she did was glance round, though, barely seeming to see it, then turned back and shrugged.

'It's not worth the bother, really. I'm in front of the engine here and that keeps me warm.'

The road ran along the banks of the Drava now, the valley around us growing progressively steeper and narrower as we left the last outlying houses behind. It's a wild, uninhabited region of southern Carinthia, with endless pine forests climbing into the mist on either side of the road. An unbroken expanse of trees, without even a single house or isolated farmstead.

Here, as during our last drive through Italy the day before, the road runs parallel to and above the river, but this felt quite different from the Isonzo. There the road is cut into the hillside, with a gently sloping lee covered in pine saplings. Here on the Drava, by contrast, the road runs along the top of a rocky embankment, with nothing but a flimsy guard rail to stop the car plunging five or ten metres over the side. From there the hill shelves steeply towards the river far below, and I could all too vividly picture my flimsy little Lancia tumbling over and over, all the way down… The river is also of an entirely different character from the Isonzo; in place of those azure meltwaters, the Drava is grey and frothy. There was something grim and menacing about the way the current, fed by melting snows, seethed along the valley floor, casting up angry billows. Uprooted trees, bits of wood and other assorted flotsam raced along in striking illustration of the river's power, and even from inside the car we could hear the roar of its roiling churn. I thought of how in ancient days, pagans saw each river as the domain or embodiment of a local spirit, and decided that the Isonzo must have been the haunt of some cheerful little nymph or river sprite, while the Drava would have been the domain of a merciless, tyrannical god. Woe to all who fall into his clutches.

With this in mind, I was driving a good deal more cautiously than usual, especially since the rain made the road slippery. We could not risk a single skid, and I noticed with alarm that even the flimsy guard rail was only present in parts; for long stretches there was nothing at all to check a car slipping over the edge. There was no other traffic on the road, and in fact we did not see another soul after leaving Klagenfurt. No traffic came from the other direction. It was just us, the mountains, the road and the river, as though we were journeying across a land that laboured under a curse. The rain made it all bleaker still. We drove on for a quarter of an hour, with no change in the landscape.

That was when I spotted a dark grey lorry in the distance, coming towards us from the direction of the Yugoslav frontier. I automatically touched the brakes. It disappeared behind a bend in the road, then reappeared. It was coming straight for us, driving on the wrong side of the road— our side—and to swerve left would have meant plunging into the void! I sounded the horn repeatedly but it made no difference; the lorry just kept coming. When we were mere seconds from one another I swerved in towards the hillside, but the oncoming lorry did likewise. I tried to right our course again, but the lorry had skidded across the road and now all but blocked it; if I hadn't stood on the brakes we would have crashed straight into it. As it was we skidded sideways ourselves, and our rear mudguard clanged against the lorry's side.

The two men in the lorry immediately jumped out, as did I, and they began shouting insults at me. They, who had been driving straight towards me on the wrong side of the road, had the temerity to claim that *I* was in the wrong! Arguing with them got me nowhere; they just kept yelling. I thought perhaps they were drunk, or else why would they be so furious? After all, their lorry was barely scratched. Neither seemed able to understand that with a few turns of the steering wheel the lorry could be straightened up and on its way again, as could we. But no, they just kept bellowing about compensation, though I could see no visible damage whatsoever to their vehicle.

Impudent scoundrels, I thought, and began in turn to lose my temper. Soon the three of us were standing hatless in the rain, roaring at one another.

That was when a big touring car pulled up behind us. The door opened, and out stepped Schönberg-Belmonte.

We were trapped!

Two accomplices were with him, one the tall, athletic

young man who had stayed in the next room to mine in Palermo, the other the hairy little man whom I first saw at the Marquis's auction. All three had pistols in their hands.

They surrounded us, while the two men from the lorry chuckled and shook their heads. I finally understood what in the adrenalin of the moment had never occurred to me: it was all a set-up designed to trap us on this deserted stretch of road.

Milolu stood by the car, her face deathly pale. Schönberg turned to her and burst out laughing.

'Did I not tell you I would never let go of what is mine?' His voice hardened, becoming harsh and peremptory. 'The painting! Give me the painting!'

I was overcome in that moment by a wave of fury the like of which I have never before experienced.

'Never! You'll never have it, you bastard!'

I wanted to throw myself on Schönberg and beat the life out of him, but three men grabbed me and held me back. Milolu's high voice cut through this noisy struggle.

'Don't hurt him! We'll give you the painting, but please don't hurt him!'

At this point my recollections grow hazy and confused. I remember Schönberg accusing Milolu of being a duplicitous bitch, of trying to double-cross him and run off with the painting. She pleaded with him, saying she had only been waiting for the right moment to hand it over. Now at last she had a chance to fulfil her promise.

It took a moment for my rage-clouded mind to process what I was hearing. She what? She was on his side? She'd been working with his gang this whole time? A moment later there seemed no doubt about it: she opened the rear door of the car and pulled back the blanket. There, right beneath it, was a large, flat package wrapped in string. The painting! She'd hidden it there, so she could hand it over the moment she had a chance! God in Heaven, she'd been secretly waiting for this very moment, knowing we would be caught!

I could hardly believe what I was seeing.

'Here it is,' she said, smiling. 'See? I'm as good as my word.'

Schönberg smirked as he took it from her. He wanted to tear the packaging from it, but Milolu laid a hand on his arm.

'Not here; the rain will damage it. Wait until you're inside.'

'Clever girl,' he said. 'Good, practical sense as well as guile. I like that.'

Then he spoke the most terrible words of all; words that cut like so many razor blades.

'You'll see; *I'm* as good as my word too. You and I will live together in Paris, just as I promised. It will be the most glorious life you can possibly imagine! Come on!'

Milolu hesitated for a moment, seeming to want to come over and say something to me first. Instead, though, she simply climbed into the big car next to Schönberg.

They drove off, and the two men from the lorry likewise got into their vehicle, reversed a little, and headed the same way. The whole thing was over in a matter of minutes, but within those few minutes my whole world had crumbled. I was alone in the pouring rain with nothing at all besides this sudden wash of pain.

Milolu!

How could she? Was she really able just to drive away, without so much as a goodbye? Taking off with an infamous gangster? Good God, it—I couldn't even think about it; the whole thing was just too monstrous. The effect of her betrayal was so crushing, in fact, that I was incapable of doing anything. Sitting down on the wheel arch, I put my head in my hands and looked down blankly at the swirling river below. Perhaps, I thought, the best thing would be simply to leap forward, and tumble to my death in the current. A few minutes and all the horror would be over.

How long I sat there I have no idea. Rain dripped down the back of my neck but I didn't notice. Making an effort to pull myself together, I tried to run over in my mind the whole three weeks or so we had spent together. Now, with the knowledge of what had transpired, a diabolical, scheming logic began to emerge in everything she had done. Seen in this light, every event and conversation only proved that I had been nothing but a tool, a useful dupe, whom this scheming trollop had manipulated with consummate, pitiless skill. She had used me to get her hands on the treasure she would need for her new life in Paris, and to get some leverage over her fellow criminal.

Yes! That was all I was to her, and nothing more! That was why she had become my lover, and practically forced me to go to the auction with her. The only reason we had taken that long, circuitous trip through Italy was to buy her time and let her drive up the price! Everything made sense now. She had presumably asked Lakatos to come from Budapest to Palermo, but he must have tried to betray her; she made sure he was arrested so that he could not disturb her carefully laid plans. When we drove to Messina it must have been Milolu who tipped them off, since how would they have known about it otherwise? I remembered now how surprised I had been when she agreed that Bodoki could accompany us from Naples to Rome. She must have been lying when she said she had never met him before; she wanted him with us, as a link between ourselves and the criminals she was selling the painting to. What about that night on the boat, which she insisted on spending in the car? Clearly a pretext, allowing her to talk to Bodoki in private and send a message by him! It was in Padua, though, that she sealed the deal with Schönberg. That was where she agreed to betray me if he promised her a life of luxury in Paris! My God, but she even told me! Not everything, of course, but she quite explicitly told me that she had made him a promise.

But how perfectly she had played her part! It was certainly enough to fool me—I had fallen for it hook, line and sinker!

What an ass! What a stupid fool! Damn it all! I had fallen for everything, though even from the first moment I met her I sensed something in her that made me uneasy. There was always some hidden part she wouldn't let me see, some mysterious quality in her smile that I could never get to the bottom of. I had thought, in spite of that part of herself she hid from me, I had thought… I thought that perhaps she really did love me. I struck my thigh with a clenched fist and almost sobbed in shame and humiliation at the idiot I had proved to be. Once or twice I had even thought that perhaps I loved her too!

These women! These heartless schemers!

This wasn't the first time I had felt this way about her, of course, but I'd been fool enough to let her wheedle her way back into my affections with a painted smile and soft, murmured apologies. I had caught her dealing with Schönberg behind my back, for God's sake! But imbecile that I am, I always believe every wide-eyed, tearful excuse. How they must laugh at me behind my back!

I write all this in relatively coherent sentences, but of course these thoughts actually rushed through my head in a confused, discordant babble, and not without the occasional note of dissension. Aside from my human instincts, which protested that some moments we had shared were simply too real and profound to have been feigned, some of the evidence didn't add up. Why, after all, had she refused the painting when I offered it to her as a gift? Wouldn't that have been easier? But that was easily explained! She would have been unable to tempt Schönberg with it unless she could show the painting's worth. First, she had to make it difficult to access, which was easier if it was in my possession, and by stealing it from me—an artist, I flatter myself, of some renown in my own right—she could more easily persuade Schönberg of its value.

All these thoughts were like hot nails driven into my skull. I kept compulsively thinking, over and over, of all the things we had done together, and each time it hurt more than the last to think that it had all been nothing but a clever scheme of hers.

My mind burned!

Still I sat there, the rain beating down relentlessly on my bare head, and gazed down at the swirling river.

And then, above the sound of the rain and the river, I gradually became conscious of a rattling motor growing steadily louder. Running a hand over my face, I looked up. It was a motorcycle, coming towards me at full speed from the direction of Klagenfurt. Just as when we saw the lorry coming towards us, the bends in the road and the high cliff kept hiding the approaching vehicle, so that it would appear for a moment, then disappear again behind the next bend. Its speed was so great, it seemed some invisible cord was dragging it towards me.

In a moment or two it was upon me, and drew up with a screech of brakes. Then the pillion rider jumped down, pulling off a leather cap and a pair of goggles.

It was Milolu.

She rushed over and threw her arms about me, kissing me with smiling tears in her eyes. In the rain it was hard to tell, but I suppose we were both crying. Between each kiss she spoke urgent, confused words.

'Thank God you're here! I got away as quick as I could—I got away!' She lowered her voice to a whisper, speaking in Hungarian, naturally. 'I told the ambulance men that you'd been in a car accident. You'll have to say the same thing!'

I had by now recovered my wits enough to take a proper look at the motorcycle, and saw that it had a large red cross painted on the side. I was still pretty shaken, though, and Milolu helped with the introductions.

'Thank goodness my husband has recovered consciousness. He banged his head in the crash and I couldn't wake him…' At the same moment she whispered in my ear, 'Give the man something and let's get out of here! They'll be after me soon!'

I hardly understood a word. Reaching into my pocket, I absent-mindedly handed the paramedic a small fortune, then we got into the car and drove off.

It's a good thing that driving a car is a bit like learning to swim. Both take a lot of concentration at first, but once you get the knack you hardly have to engage your brain at all.

We reached the Yugoslav border without further mishap, but I was so dazed that I have no real recollection of the crossing. There was one customs checkpoint on the Austrian side and one on the Yugoslav side, but both went quickly enough, and we were on the road again within half an hour. We sped on towards Marburg. Milolu tried to explain her escape, but I was having difficulty enough concentrating on the road and barely heard what she said.

An official sent by Rudić was waiting for us on the edge of the town, and he escorted us to my friend's villa. We were extremely warmly received upon our arrival.

He, like me, is a bachelor, and—though a little fuller of figure than when I last saw him—still basically the same sort of good-natured bohemian he always was. There are several fine guest rooms in his villa, and without making any prurient inquiries he made sure our rooms were directly beside one another. Only once—when he was showing us our bathroom—did I catch a mischievous gleam in his eyes.

'There's only one bathroom up here, so I'm afraid you'll have to share,' he said with a smile. Nothing else showed the slightest sign of his guessing why we might be travelling together.

After a splendid meal—and even better wine—I outlined the Schönberg business, telling him everything that had happened to us from Palermo until Marburg. Only when it came to Milolu's escape from Schönberg was I at a loss, and since she had already gone to bed we could hardly ask. I also admitted that the primary reason for this impromptu visit was the hope that we would be safer here than in a hotel.

Rudić reassured me. His villa was surrounded by a high iron fence, and the town police station stood at the corner of the street. He even telephoned them and asked them to keep a close eye on the street outside as a favour.

'I'll make other arrangements tomorrow,' he promised as we said goodnight.

Up in my room, I found everything already laid out for me. Milolu had unpacked our things while I stayed downstairs talking. My pyjamas were on the bed, and fresh linen was laid out on the sofa. My sponge bag was sitting on the desk in the corner.

There was something else, though: leaning against the mirror stood precisely the same wide, flat package wrapped up in paper which I thought I had seen her hand over to Schönberg that very afternoon. It was the Leonardo!

Flabbergasted, I snatched it up and rushed over to Milolu's room.

'What's this? How did you manage to get it back?'

Already in bed, she smiled sweetly at me.

'Oh Tibor, surely you didn't think I'd actually give it to him?'

With careful fingers she unfastened the string, then pulled back the paper and wadding to reveal the masterpiece beneath. Then she handed it back to me.

'But—how? How in…'

So she told me, explaining that in a little shop in Padua she had found a portrait of Victor Emmanuel in inlaid wood, with proportions almost identical to those of the Leonardo. It was this portrait—which, she confessed with a wistful sigh, she had been unaccountably fond of—that was in the package she had handed over to Schönberg.

'Il Re Liberatore' indeed!

For some time she had been on the lookout for a package of similar dimensions to the painting, lest our pursuers should succeed in waylaying us. Her hope had been in the haste with which criminals always act in such moments: they would not want to hang about, unwrapping and rewrapping packages. That was why she had kept it under the blanket, so as to have it close to hand in case of emergencies.

'Of course, it was absurdly dangerous, and I'd never have done it except as a last resort. Remember how Schönberg wanted to look at it straight away? Thank goodness it was raining; I don't think I'd have been able to stop him otherwise, and if he'd opened it on the spot then of course that would have been the end of us. He'd have thrown us both into that ravine, then taken the case out of the boot and tipped the car down after us. On our way back to Klagenfurt I asked him what he would have done if I hadn't given him the picture, and that's more or less what he said. He also added this: "I always do a thorough job, and it's easy to fake a good car crash. People often get thrown from the vehicle on the way down anyway, so there is no way to tell the difference afterwards." That's why I had to go with him. If I'd stayed with you then he'd have opened it in the car, but while I was with him it never occurred to him to doubt its authenticity. He took me back into Klagenfurt. Straight back to the hotel we stayed in, actually. When we got out he left me in the lobby, saying he had to pay his men first. That was a stroke of luck! I had to get out of there before he realised I'd swapped the pictures.

'I remembered noticing when we stayed there that there is an emergency exit through the bathroom, which is also where they bring in the bigger pieces of luggage. I didn't want to go out through the main entrance, since who could tell what guard Schönberg might have posted? It worked, in any case, and I soon found myself alone on the street. I just ran blindly for a few hundred yards, then stopped; I honestly had no idea what to do next, or how to get back to you. That's when it struck me: an ambulance! I asked the way to the hospital from the first person I met, and sprinted over. You can imagine the state of me, out of breath and panicked, with hair plastered to the side of my face. I hardly had to fake distress! In a very bad sort of German I made them understand that we had been in an accident somewhere out along the Drava road, and that you were unconscious; I forgot the word for concussion but that's what I wanted to say. I had come straight here for help, I said, and we had to get back there at once!

'They had a motorcycle ready, and I told the man—untruthfully, of course—that I knew how to ride pillion. I climbed on the back and we set off. Well, you know what these big motorcycles are like; we were absolutely flying, and I don't think any car in the world could have overtaken us. That's how I got back to you.'

That was her story, and I was astounded at the danger she had knowingly put herself in. I've been under fire before and not run, but what she did shows a kind of courage which I suspect only women possess. The sheer audacity of it! I took her in my arms and thought of everything that had gone through my head as I sat in the rain and looked down into the river. I felt terrible shame: while I sat there cursing her as a faithless, scheming strumpet, she had been risking her life! How could I ever have doubted her? I didn't say I word of all this, though; I just held her in my arms and covered her hair with kisses, since as soon as she finished speaking she buried her face against my shoulder.

It took me a few minutes to realise that she was crying. She had, in fact, dissolved into tears, and great, heaving sobs began to shake her body, growing steadily stronger. Now, after it was all over, she was finally able to release the terror and loathing from inside her.

'Darling,' I said, 'why are you crying? Don't cry, darling, it's all over now. Everything's all right now. The danger's passed and we're together again…'

Her hands went up my arm and touched my shoulders, then my neck. Then she ran her hands over my face, as if wishing to check that it was really me and that I was really there. At length, her tears subsided. She still shook, but I eventually realised that it was from a combination of tears and laughter. I pulled back and looked at her with mock sternness.

'Is that chortling I hear?'

She looked up at me, and though her eyes were still wet with tears, she grinned broadly.

'I was thinking of Schönberg's face when he pulls off the paper and wadding and sees, instead of a Leonardo da Vinci, Signore Ristorini's inlaid-wood portrait of Victor Emmanuel II. Poor Uncle Schöni will be beside himself!'

I laughed too, and kissed her passionately. In a moment I forgot everything we had been through during the day: all the worry, danger, fear and pain dissolved in the meeting of our bodies, as when some uneasy D minor interlude is swept away by a triumphant return of the main theme.

I was in the middle of shaving the next morning when Rudić came in to tell me some interesting news. It turns out that last night he called the police in Klagenfurt and asked them to check whether a French citizen by the name of Schönberg-Belmonte was presently staying in town and if so, where. Half an hour later they called back to say that a man of that name had indeed stayed in the town but had departed that evening on the Tauernbahn Express. In all probability he wanted to catch the Arlberg Express in Salzburg, since he had asked the hotel porter about the connections there.

He was gone!

Rudić had more news, though: he said that Schönberg, together with two other men, had apparently come to Marburg on the morning of the day before yesterday. He and one of his friends had returned to Austria after the expiry of their one-day visas. The third man, who had a Hungarian passport, had either stayed in Yugoslavia or travelled on somewhere else.

This was already a good quantity of news to deal with, but my host was not finished yet. He also said that last night, in a tavern on the outskirts of town, an unknown young man had tried to kill himself. He shot himself, but his aim was not quite true. Though still alive, the copious blood-loss meant that he remained unconscious and it was impossible to question him. He had left no note, nor any money or baggage anywhere in town. Indeed, he appeared to have nothing in the world besides the clothes on his back and that little Browning pistol.

'He's in the hospital now. Tomorrow the border guards are going to take a look at him, but the general belief is that he's the third man in the group that came over with Schönberg. His name is signed in the border papers in a pretty illegible scrawl, but it seems to be written as either Endre Bodoli or Bodoki, and that's why I came to see you so early. We should go over to the hospital at once and see him, since in all probability it's the same Bodoki you told me about last night. If it is, then his evidence will be important.'

I dressed quickly and we headed to the hospital. We found the patient in an isolation ward; they wanted no unauthorised visitors to have contact with him. The nurse told us that this morning he had regained some sort of consciousness but was still very weak. We went in anyway, and I knew at once that it was indeed Bodoki. He was lying in bed with his eyes closed, and I assumed at first that he was sleeping. I began speaking quietly to Rudić, but Bodoki soon opened his eyes. He looked at me with a wild mixture of hope and despair.

'You're—you're the *maestro* aren't you…?' He raised a weak arm to gesture at the seat next to him. 'I want to—to tell you something—just you…'

Rudić made a sign that he would leave us, and I sat down next to the stricken man. Hoping to put him at ease, I tried to avoid the solemnity usual at such moments.

'Now why would a clever boy like you do a stupid thing like this?'

He brushed this aside with a feeble flutter of his left hand.

'What was stupid was—was missing the mark. I should have…'

There was silence for a few minutes, then he went on.

'It was me who did it. I stole the painting. I—I was in trouble for embezzling money from the time when I was a clerk. I didn't actually embezzle any myself, but I borrowed from the man who did. Borrowed a lot. I thought it was his,

208

though; I didn't know it was stolen. They were going to stick me in prison if I didn't pay it all back. Accomplice, that's what they called me. But how could I get the money? That's when I met Schönberg...'

His eyes closed and he was silent for a long time. I thought he had finished, and was just getting ready to rise when he spoke again.

'He promised everything. Exotic foreign cities, glamorous women, the easy life... And what a bloody idiot I was! Then he brought me here. I was in his power, see? I could hardly do anything without his orders. Then he—he just left me here. He just wanted rid of me...'

The poor little devil began to sob.

Now I was the one wanting more; I wanted details. How was it that he didn't even have so much as a passport or an overnight bag?

'He—he brought me here, then took away everything so I couldn't leave. Then he told me he'd already informed Budapest that I stole the picture and that the police would be here within a day to arrest me. All he left me was—was the gun. He knew I'd rather die than go to prison; I even said so once...'

He fell silent and I began to wonder if there was any way I could help the poor man. After all, he wasn't the real criminal, just a weak, easily led sort of fellow. I advised him to turn himself in. It would be recorded as a voluntary confession, and that would significantly reduce his sentence, especially if he cooperated in the search for Schönberg. I was quite certain that Schönberg had been lying when he said he had informed Budapest about his involvement in the theft, and said as much. He would still have to do some time in prison, I hastened to add, but with all the extenuating circumstances—including this pitiable suicide attempt—I found it hard to imagine a sentence of more than a year. If he submitted to his lawful punishment then I promised him that afterwards, so long as *he* promised to live a decent, law-abiding life, I would see to it that he was employed in a good job. He is, after all, not without talent.

He looked at me, gratitude shining in his eyes. 'You'd— really do that for me?' He took a deep breath, then sighed. 'All right. I'll do everything just as you say.'

We said goodbye and I extended my hand. He hesitated for a moment, then shook it feebly. Two tears rolled down his cheeks.

I told Rudić everything, and he said he would come by later to oversee the taking of Bodoki's confession. Then we went back to the villa, where a magnificent late breakfast awaited us. At length, our appetites sated, we said our goodbyes and set off.

Just the two of us, heading home at last.

Milolu and I. Just the two of us, happy and alone, and heading for Hungary!

X

Tibor Vida's return of the stolen Leonardo da Vinci to the Budapest Fine Arts Museum was a sensational triumph. Though he had wanted Milla to come with him, he ended up going alone, since she categorically refused any part in it.

Not for the world!

He kept telling her that it was she and not he who had rescued this stolen artwork, but she was adamant.

'This is your painting, Mr Vida.'

Now that the adventure was over and they were back in bourgeois Budapest, they were trying to put aside some of the precipitous overfamiliarity which had developed between them on the road.

'You bought it, not me. It's really nothing to do with me.'

Nothing to do with me? Unbelievable!

The reader may share Tibor's view that—while modesty is a noble and admirable trait—this was rather stretching it.

The return of the painting was, of course, greeted with jubilation at the Museum. Everyone employed in the building came as soon as they heard the news, and old Behr rushed over at once.

A single glance was enough, and he smiled broadly.

'This is it, all right. The real thing!'

The Director phoned the Home Secretary to share the

news. The minister was, naturally, delighted, but could not resist claiming some small part of the glory for himself.

'I knew it would turn up before long. I made a very generous offering at a shrine to St Anthony of Padua, and can honestly say I've never once been disappointed when I beg his intercession.'

He also insisted that the whole affair remain *strictly* under wraps.

'We've kept it secret this long, and I don't see any reason why it shouldn't stay that way. Let's quietly put back the painting and say no more about it. If anyone found out that it took some damned opera composer to rescue one of our most precious heirlooms, those dogs in the opposition would be baying for blood! And they'd want to know why we kept it secret for so long! No, the government isn't so strong that it could withstand a national embarrassment of that sort. They'd come for you too, my dear man, don't think they wouldn't! I'm saying this for your sake as well as mine. The truth is, I treat anyone serving under me as I would my own son, and do everything in my power to protect them, but it would be beyond even *my* considerable influence to save you if this business came out.'

An implied threat lurked behind his words, and the Director was shrewd enough to recognise it. Still, he said, it wouldn't do for Tibor Vida's achievement to go entirely unrewarded.

'Naturally, naturally. I have to say I admire what he did

greatly. Shows pluck and all that. What I'll do is this. At the next cabinet meeting I'll propose that we award him the Order of Merit, Second Class, but officially say that it's for "Services to Art outside Hungary". That description covers it, I should think, but it's vague enough that there won't be any uncomfortable questions.'

'Shall I ask if he'll accept it? He's here at the Museum now.'

'Ask if he'll accept it? Good grief, man, what is there to ask? It's just about the highest honour that can be awarded to a civilian and it's never been given to a musician before! I'm making a very great exception in view of the circumstances. Tell him, though, that he's not to speak to anyone about this business of the picture! The whole deal's off if he goes to the press. Do you understand? That's an absolutely necessary precondition!'

That was the end of the conversation. The Director communicated the Home Secretary's strict demands for secrecy, and Tibor accepted them willingly; after all, he had promised much the same to Milla, who did not want her own name to come up in relation to the painting.

In spite of this, the disappearance and miraculous reappearance of the famous Leonardo did not remain a secret for long; too many people knew about it by now. All the employees of the Museum for a start, and all the technicians and artisans who had been working there when it was stolen. Many border officials, government functionaries and policemen knew, and though they were forbidden from discussing it in public, nothing could prevent them talking about it among themselves.

There were others, too. All the editorial staff at *Az Est* knew, as did their correspondents in Rome. Something known by so many people is not destined to remain a secret for long, especially in such a city—can there be a people on earth more addicted to gossip than the inhabitants of Budapest?—and though the papers never printed a word, it was not long before everyone knew all about it.

This was the outcome of all the Home Secretary's stern injunctions about secrecy.

To explain what followed, however, we'll have to leap ahead, about five or six weeks into the future. That was when a backbencher from the opposition party rose and demanded an official explanation from the Home Secretary regarding the widely known theft of an artwork from the Budapest Fine Arts Museum.

The Home Secretary immediately washed his hands of the whole affair, pinning the blame squarely on the Museum's director. This provoked no uproar and for a time it seemed that the Home Secretary would emerge with no damage to his reputation.

The Director, however, was not willing to see his good name casually tarnished with an insinuation of professional negligence, and immediately launched a merciless counterattack against his former mentor. The uncle of the son-in-law of the second cousin of the Regent of Hungary was a good friend of his, and indeed it was to this—comparatively straightforward—chain of patronage that he owed his position at the Museum. He put the wheels of this great machine in motion and within a few days a letter in the elegant script of the nation's Regent reached the offices of the Home Secretary. Amid much talk of 'your esteemed and honourable services to your country' and 'after careful examination of all the relevant circumstances', the Home Secretary was kindly invited to resign his position.

There is after all, at least occasionally, some justice in the world.

The criminal investigation, meanwhile, continued apace. Bodoki's confession was submitted and the Yugoslav government promptly extradited him to Hungary. He was placed in custody. In the end, however, he was released without trial: legal experts agreed that sentencing would undoubtedly be lenient on account of the extenuating circumstances, and he had already undergone most of what could be expected in pre-trial detention.

Lakatos, meanwhile, was also released from prison in Italy, when the Hungarian police at last sent a high-ranking official to Rome to plead for him. The focus of the Italian investigation had in any case switched to Schönberg and his gang, especially since extensive tests had shown no evidence of Lakatos's fingerprints on the package of anti-fascist material. Knowing that Schönberg was now a wanted man throughout half of Europe, they hoped to arrest him first.

The Hungarian police were equally determined, however, and since Lakatos was the only person on the force to have met Schönberg personally, he was dispatched to Paris at once. And there, like a bloodhound loosed from his cage, he is tirelessly at work in pursuit of his quarry. There have, as yet, been no arrests, but with such dedicated professionals on the case we have reason to hope that Schönberg will soon receive his just punishment. All the same, nothing can be taken for granted when it comes to a man of his ruthless intelligence and financial resources.

That is how matters stand at present.

Which is all very well, I hear the reader exclaim, but what about Milla Anderson?

Well, that is another story entirely, and Tibor Vida tells it best.

From the Diary of Tibor Vida

Budapest, 16ᵗʰ of April
I haven't written a word in this diary since we got back. There hasn't been much to say, and in any case I haven't been in the mood. Somehow those three weeks on the road feel like a different world, with no possible connection to my life here.

The whole thing was dangerous, difficult, and unbelievably hard on my nerves, but it was exhilarating too. Spending so much time together with that remarkable woman… To be with her always, day and night, paying attention to a thousand tiny details: the way she walks, or sits down in a chair, or presses her palms together and props her chin on splayed fingers. They way that smile illuminates her face when I put my arms around her, her lips parting with a flash of white teeth. And then there was the lovemaking, the tension steadily mounting like urgent, rising dissonances, before at last dissolving in a shared major chord of climax and resolution. It was, if I'm honest, quite unlike anything I've ever experienced with anyone else. I realised, in fact, that I had never really shared my life with anyone before her, and never understood how magical it could be. To have her warmth, her femininity, her subtle fragrance around me always…

But that's all over now. We still meet, of course—in fact, I've seen her almost every day since we got back.

Almost every day, but not quite. Sometimes a day goes by when we don't meet, and on one occasion two. It's different now, since of course I'm a busy man, and we have to schedule a time and a place. Perhaps we only have time for a quick coffee, and I'm forced to watch the clock the whole time.

If I visit her it has to be during the day, with no chance of anything besides tea and conversation, since it turns out that she doesn't have her own place, but lives in the spare room of her aunt's apartment. If she visits me then it also has to be during the day: I'm staying at the Ritz, and it would stir up all sorts of gossip if she stayed the night. After all, I've become something of a minor celebrity, and I have no wish to ruin her reputation. All the same, I'd give a lot for the chance of one long, happy night in her arms…

Work takes up a lot of her time as well, since she's writing a series of articles on 'modern Italy'. It's basically a series of interesting or humorous vignettes based on the things she saw there, and turns out to be the reason she was in Italy in the first place, when we first met. She read a few of them aloud to me, and she's really a very talented writer. There's one about the little man Pancia who ran the Albergo del Paradiso, and another about the woodworker who made the portrait of Victor Emmanuel.

And here I am, tugged this way and that by endless social engagements, and meetings with lawyers or publishers. What an ungodly waste of time!

A few days ago I looked up Endre Miklós, the owner and editor-in-chief of *Az Est*. He's an old friend of mine, and championed my music back in the early days. I wanted to tell him everything Milolu had done to get the Leonardo home safely, so at least somebody would know the truth. He was her employer, after all, and I wanted him to know what a clever, brave—perhaps even foolhardy—journalist he has at his disposal.

He met me in his editorial office, since he now oversees the entire journalistic output personally. I had plenty to say, and ended up talking for a very long time. When I had finished, he looked at me in silence for a few moments with those big, protuberant eyes of his. Then he smiled.

'She's certainly a remarkable woman. Tell me, why don't you ask her to marry you?'

Ask her *what*? Somehow the thought had never entered my head. I'm not sure what stammered response I gave, but probably something along the lines of being too old and decrepit for anything of that sort. Then I quickly made my excuses and hurried off.

That was when I clearly saw the danger I was running. Marry? Tie myself down? Every instinct shuddered at the prospect. What would become of me? Always expected home on time, asked to give an account of where I had been and who I had seen... I haven't had any such obligations to anyone since I first left home, and the idea of someone having a rightful—indeed legal—claim upon me felt intolerable. Then there was the prospect of children within a year or two, with their own irrefutable claims on my time and attention. No! An ordinary man might willingly shoulder such burdens, but an artist? Never!

It would also mean abandoning all those little romantic adventures, any thrilling encounters which might chance to come along in the future. After all, it's those unexpected moments, the sudden flushes of desire, that make life worth living. Then again... There was still that voice at the back of my mind, whispering that all the 'adventures' I had enjoyed to this point, and might enjoy in the future, were tawdry, cheap and commonplace when compared to the emotions I had experienced with Milolu.

That's not all, though; there's something more serious. I'm forty-five years old now and she's barely over thirty. That's a hell of an age gap! Soon I really will be an old man, whereas she'll be a young woman for a long time yet. I don't want to impose that on her, and what if she begins to resent her increasingly frail partner? What if she seeks affection with a younger, fitter lover?

No! I couldn't bear it! The best thing, as I've said all along, is to end things straight away. Meeting every day like this probably just prolongs the inevitable, making our eventual split all the harder. In any case, I don't want to spoil the magical beauty of those three weeks by mingling my memories of her with a lot of humdrum encounters in noisy Budapest cafés. Better to keep those memories apart, a treasure among my recollections.

Yes, that's definitely the wisest move.

I have to! I will. I'll gradually prepare myself, then—what? Perhaps I'd better go abroad again. A trip to America may be on the cards in any case, since my agent has been corresponding with a big New York theatre for some weeks now. Going away for a few months would mean a natural end to our relationship, since by the time I got back I imagine

I would be with someone else. And what about her? Well, she hasn't taken holy orders, has she? So presumably she'd be—well, with someone else. Of course she would.

I have to get away from here before that happens!

18th of April
The chance for a trip away came sooner than I thought, though to Berlin rather than America. The hundredth German performance of *Shakuntala* is coming up and they asked me to conduct the orchestra at a special gala event to mark the occasion. They offered a rather pretty package, actually. I'd stay in a nice hotel for a week and conduct two rehearsals, then the big event itself.

The whole thing sounded ideal and I accepted at once. The money is good too, of course, but that isn't what tempted me. I accepted it because a week away is a perfect 'trial separation' for us. I'll be busy the entire time and it will get me used to life on my own again. Here I just sit around thinking about her all day, and though my big Steinway grand sits in the corner with a blank sheet of music paper on the stand, I don't get a minute's work done. I should sit down and focus on my music, but instead I just pine after her. In the morning I hope she'll ring me, in the afternoon I hope she'll drop by to see me, and in the evening I hope I'll run into her in some bar or theatre. Things can't go on like this, and it will only end if I made a decisive, deliberate break. The problem is, in my present state of mind I'm not sure I'm strong enough for that. A bit of time away will do me good. We leave a week on Saturday, nine days from now.

I told Milolu about my forthcoming trip this afternoon, and she said it sounded like a wonderful idea. She's a very intelligent woman, after all, and knows much better than to cling to a man. In fact, she really did seem delighted at the news, more as you'd expect from a good friend than a former lover.

A little too delighted, if I'm honest.

I wonder why? Why would she be so pleased at my going away? Does she have something else up her sleeve? Could she be looking for some way to be rid of me? Has she already found someone younger and better looking?

This thought flashed through my mind, but I rather doubt it. No, she's a passionate woman, but I don't believe finding a man has ever been her first priority. People who've known her for a long time say she's never had a serious attachment, apart from that abortive marriage in America. Perhaps it's something else. Maybe she's as conscious as I am of how banal our interactions have become since we got back from Italy, and I dare say she's as capable as I am of judging that it's better to end things sooner rather than later. I never heard her say as much, but then of course she's never been one to pour her heart out.

Somehow it's her intelligence which reassures me. She really is singularly intelligent, in a way I don't think I've ever encountered before in anyone. And yes, the thought of it comforts me. And when I think... Ah! Forget it! I hate it when my brain starts off like this!

19th of April, morning
I hardly slept last night but just lay there tossing and turning. This big empty bed! I keep thinking of all those nights when we lay in one another's arms, snuggled close to one another yet sound asleep, like wild beasts in the jungle.

I counted up all the days since I first met her, and found to my astonishment that it barely amounts to a month and a half! It feels as though she's been part of my life for an eternity... I walked my recollections back, back to the transformative, ecstatic moment when she pulled up on a motorcycle; the moment I realised she had come back to me. Then back to the first time we spoke, looking at that advertisement for the Marquis Bentiruba's auction. She since confessed that she stood next to me in the conscious hope that I would strike up a conversation. What a power is femininity! Able to draw one wordlessly towards it through—what? Some faint scent, perhaps, or simply the sheer magnetism of her presence.

Irresistible.

These wretched memories!

I should drop in at the Museum; I still haven't seen our painting since it was restored to its place in the gallery. I feel somehow obliged to say a last goodbye to old Leonardo too, since in a sense it was he who brought us together. That painting is responsible for those three wonderful, terrifying weeks, which in sum probably add up to the happiest period of my adult life.

That's where my goodbyes should begin.

The same day, afternoon
That Leonardo! Dear God, that marvellous bloody Leonardo! I've just come back from there, and… Well, I had better start from the beginning.

I went to the Museum and, not knowing the place, asked one of the security guards for directions. He told me where to go: I had to pass through two rooms to a third, smaller room at the end. Here a single painting hung against wallpaper of green velvet, mounted in an exquisite gold frame: the *Head of Christ* by Leonardo.

In front of it was a long bench, upholstered in black leather, and sitting on it was a young, dark-haired woman.

Milolu.

She had come here too, to look at the painting. She was sitting with her elbows propped on her knees and her chin resting on her palms, gazing in rapt, motionless wonder.

It was impossible to say how long she'd been there, but it could have been a very long time. She did not hear my footsteps, nor even notice when I sat down next to her. She just kept gazing at the painting.

'Milolu?' I said softly. 'Milolu? You came here as well?'

She turned to me, and I saw with surprise that her eyes were full of tears. She looked at me with a doleful expression, and though her red lips parted, no sound emerged.

I threw my arms about her.

'Milolu!'

We kissed, and our lips remained together for a long time. This was no kiss of hot passion, though, at least not for me. This was a kiss of love, a kiss of union.

Parting at last, she cuffed at her eyes and looked at me, then finally spoke. Her words were quiet and slow.

'I was just thinking back. The only reason this is here is… I wasn't crying, you shouldn't think that. I do understand, you know. I understand that you have to go. You have your profession, your livelihood—I know. You didn't say it, but I know. I know that you're going because—to make it clean, to separate cleanly, so we can still be friends. You're a successful artist, Tibor, and you've got your own world. A serious relationship isn't right for a man in your trade. What would you need a wife for?'

Her voice became quieter still.

'I just wanted to say that I'll always be grateful, and that I'll treasure my memories of those three weeks. I'm grateful I was able to spend them with you.'

These words were so heartfelt, at once so affecting yet so unaffected, that I was simply unable to bear it.

'But Milolu! That isn't what I want at all!'

She shook her head and smiled with puffy eyes.

'My sweet Tibor; maybe I see our situation more clearly than you. Those three weeks with you in Italy were the happiest of my life, but this? Creeping about, meeting for a stolen hour or two here and there? Constantly pretending to have an interview with you, or some other stupid pretext? I can't keep doing that for long. It's not in my nature. I wasn't born to be anyone's secret lover. Not even yours.' She raised a hand as though to shoo away the very idea, then went on. 'No! Better to end it all now and make a clean break. Don't worry about me, I'll manage all right…'

All at once I was struck by the sheer magnitude of what I would lose if this woman disappeared from my life. I did not want her as a lover, I wanted to share my life with her, now and forever. Where else would I ever find anyone who understood me so well? Who loved me so deeply?

Suddenly it was all so clear to me.

I love her.

What was I to do? Well, marry her of course! What else could I do?

The minute I made this decision I felt a great wave of joy crash over me. I wrapped her in my arms again, whispering not into her ear but into her mouth.

'Well then I'll just have to marry you, won't I? Will you be my wife?'

Her arms embraced me tightly and we kissed for a long time, then she pulled back and looked at me.

'And you won't be cross?'

'Cross? Me? But Milolu, when have I ever been cross?'

She burst out laughing, then pressed her mouth against my cheek.

'You've never been cross, and I'll see to it that you're never cross again.'

Now it was my turn to speak.

'Let's go straight down to the City Hall; they can marry us there without all the fuss of an official proclamation. Then we can go to Berlin together as man and wife.'

We stood up, then walked over to stand in front of the Leonardo. This was still a goodbye, but now a happy, hopeful one.

More than goodbye, though, a word of thanks also seemed in order. Neither of us said as much, but I'm sure both of us felt it. The painting brought us together, and through it our love had begun. It had accompanied us on all our travels, and become a sort of old friend, wordlessly watching over us. We stood looking at it for a long time, and the truth is that I was deeply, deeply moved.

Then, hand in hand, we walked away, but not before stopping in the doorway for one last look back.

The gold frame glowed bright, and in that moment it was as though the head of Christ lived, his sublime features bestowing upon us a final blessing.

Kolozsvár, 28th of June 1949

227

Afterword

In the summer of 1949, Miklós Bánffy wrote to tell his sister that he was working on a novella. 'Its title is *Milolu*...most of the events take place in Fascist Italy and I shall try to depict the conditions of that time since I travelled in Sicily then and was able to observe many things...At least it makes me forget the countless problems hanging around my neck.'

Those problems were enormous and began in mid-October of 1944, when a pall of dark smoke rose above the Transylvanian village of Bonchida. A wing of the great country house of the Bánffy family was aflame. How and why the fire started remains a mystery. The owner, Count Miklós Bánffy, was far away in Budapest. With no one in charge, the flames were able to spread and soon the entire edifice was burning. There seemed to be no way of stopping the destruction.

The house had been used as a field hospital by the German army until a few days before the fire broke out. The Germans had been ordered to evacuate westwards. The hospital was emptied of its staff and wounded; the most valuable contents of the house were also taken along, 'for safe-keeping'. Some forty wagons laden with paintings, furniture, silverware and porcelain left for the Reich. The train made it as far as Slovakia, where it was apparently destroyed by Allied or Soviet bombing. Or perhaps not. Who knows?

Once the fire burned itself out, the looters appeared, to take what could still be taken from the few rooms which remained intact. Bits of furniture, china, window frames, shutters, doors, anything would do. The few books which survived out of a library once containing twenty-seven thousand volumes were of no interest to anyone. Dumped unceremoniously in a muddy courtyard, these rare and ancient tomes made it easier for carts, heavy with loot, to make their way to the entrance gate. Documents from the archives fared no better. Most ended up in the stream which ran through the park surrounding the house. Letters, decrees, rescripts signed by princes, kings and emperors were seen floating in the water for days, until some remnants could finally be rescued by a few intrepid archivists from Kolozsvár/Cluj.

Seventy years earlier, in December 1873, when Miklós Bánffy was born, all of this lay in a distant and unimaginable future. Then, the great house at Bonchida was living through its last golden age. The house itself was a typical Transylvanian amalgam of every architectural style since the Middle Ages and yet somehow managed to present an image of timeless dignity, grandeur and unity. The triumphant griffins of the Bánffys greeted visitors above the entrance gate, while the great semicircular stables were embellished by more than three dozen sculptures depicting characters from ancient Greek mythology. Their restless Baroque energy brought a touch of southern Italy to the eastern marches of central Europe.

Inside the house, at the top of the imposing main staircase, doors opened into the stuccoed great hall, used as a dining room. Then followed reception room after reception room: the blue salon with a portrait of Count Dénes Bánffy by Martin van Meytens, Maria Theresa's court painter; the yellow salon; the Maria Theresa salon, with its fine late eighteenth-century Viennese furniture. The billiard room was the repository of family portraits and much of the old Transylvanian nobility was represented on its walls. The library, housed in the northwest tower and decorated in Empire style, contained only a small portion of the vast collection of books which had been assembled over the centuries.

Then there was the garden: over seven hundred acres laid out in the English style. Well-tended paths led though lawns and flower beds. An ornamental lake, often used by Bánffy and his sister for boating, was fed by an arm of the Szamos river which meandered slowly through the park, criss-crossed by elegant little white bridges. Deeper within the garden, dark, forbidding pines predominated, creating the impression that one had strayed into a wild Transylvanian forest—though one created not by nature but by artifice.

As in most country houses of this size in Europe, there were multitudes of servants and here, as elsewhere, there was a pecking order. At the summit of this hierarchy stood the educated foreigners who were engaged to teach languages to the children. They tended to be impecunious or adventurous men and women from western Europe, principally France and England. Among those who served at Bonchida, one stands out: Edward Willford. Though some accounts describe him as a teacher of English, my father—Bánffy's nephew—remembered him as a butler, a distinguished bearded gentleman held in affectionate esteem by the family. One of the earliest portraits Miklós Bánffy ever painted was of the much respected 'Edward'.

The lord and master of this miniature court was Miklós Bánffy's father, Count George Bánffy. The largest landowner (some seventy-five thousand acres) and the highest taxpayer in Transylvania, he was also the scion of an ancient family. The Bánffys could prove documentary descent from the middle of the 12th century but they claimed to go back much further: the Pecheneg chieftain Tomizoba, who accompanied the Magyar leader Árpád in his conquest of Hungary at the end of the ninth century, was said to have been the ancestor of all living Bánffys. Miklós Bánffy himself was often called 'the Pecheneg' behind his back by his enemies, both literary and political. He rather enjoyed it. As he would have enjoyed—had he known—a French diplomat's reference to him as a 'cunning Mongol' in a secret dispatch. There was a certain irony in this given that one of Bánffy's earliest recorded ancestors had died fighting those very same Mongols at the battle of Muhi in 1241.

George Bánffy returned home from his Grand Tour of western Europe at the age of twenty-six, ready to settle down and marry. His choice fell upon Baroness Irma Bánffy, his cousin and neighbour. By all accounts this was not a customary arranged marriage but a genuine love match. Their daughter, Katinka (my grandmother), was born in 1871, followed by a son, Miklós, two years later. The rejoicing at the birth of an heir would soon be replaced by sorrow: Irma Bánffy died suddenly in 1875. She was only twenty-three. Miklós could have had but little memory of his mother. His father, inconsolable, never re-married.

Life at Bonchida must have seemed remote and possibly tedious for the two half-orphans. But it was not static. The family usually spent a month or two at their town house in Kolozsvár, and the winter in the so-called Palace District of Budapest. There, two of Miklós Bánffy's aunts, Countess Anna Zichy and Countess Clarisse Károlyi, went out of their way to provide the maternal comfort that may have been lacking at home. Relations with the Károlyi family were especially close because the two Károlyi cousins, Mihály and Erzsébet, were almost the same age and—like the young Bánffys—had also lost their mother. A third aunt, Elise, opened a window on another world for the children. Elise Bánffy had married Count Richard Berchtold, whose mother owned Palazzo Contarini degli Scrigni on the Grand Canal in Venice. Bánffy, having stayed there often, became a great admirer of Italian culture and spoke Italian well. He also formed friendships in Italy which would later stand him in good stead.

Miklós studied law in Kolozsvár and Budapest. Though he may have taken greater pleasure in the painting lessons he received from Bertalan Székely, a famous artist of the nineteenth-century Hungarian school, he was nevertheless destined for a political career. He became a member of the Hungarian Parliament in 1901 and Lord-Lieutenant of Kolozs County five years later. However, he had also begun to write and publish under the name Miklós Kisbán (the pseudonym fooled few people). His play *The Great Lord* (*A Nagyúr*), about Attila the Hun, was favourably reviewed, even by critics not generally sympathetic to the literary efforts of the aristocracy. His political and artistic commitments tied him increasingly to Budapest and he spent less time in Bonchida. Meanwhile his sister married Tamás Barcsay and went to live at Gyalu, not far from Kolozsvár.

Alongside his literary achievements, Bánffy made great contributions to the field of music. In 1912 he was appointed intendant of the Royal Hungarian Opera, a role he took up with enthusiasm. He decided to reduce the emphasis on German works and introduce new operas from France, Italy—and Hungary. In 1918 he undertook the staging of Bartók's only opera, *Bluebeard's Castle*. The music was difficult and radical but Bánffy and his Italian conductor Egisto Tango cajoled the musicians into performing and Bánffy designed the sets and costumes.

Nearly two years before, Bánffy had taken on a task which was as much artistic as political. The emperor Franz Joseph had died in 1916, after a reign of 68 years. His successor, Charles IV, had to be crowned King of Hungary before the end of the year for a variety of political, constitutional and fiscal reasons. Bánffy was charged with overseeing the artistic aspects of the coronation ceremony. He gathered around him an outstanding team of architects, artists and craftsmen. Seamstresses and carpenters worked around the clock under his direction. In the end, the event was a remarkable success—and it was to be the swan song of an ancient monarchy. Less than two years later, under the weight of defeat, the old order collapsed and was replaced by a revolutionary government headed by Mihály Károlyi, Bánffy's cousin and erstwhile playmate. The two men were in completely opposing political camps: Bánffy submitted his resignation from the Opera.

Hungary in the meantime descended into chaos. Large parts of the old kingdom were occupied by Serbian, Czechoslovak and Romanian troops. Bonchida and Gyalu were both now in occupied territory. In Budapest, Károlyi's government, under pressure from all sides, fell in March 1919 and was replaced by a revolutionary regime dominated by Communists. The latter survived only for four months. Stability was finally restored early in 1920, with the election of Admiral Miklós Horthy as regent. Bánffy decided to re-enter political life. In April 1921 he was appointed

Foreign Minister. Promising negotiations with Edvard Beneš regarding the largely Hungarian-populated parts of southern Slovakia, assigned to Czechoslovakia by the Paris Peace Conference, came to nothing after King Charles IV attempted for the second time to reclaim the Hungarian throne. The Czechoslovaks declared that they were prepared to prevent a royal restoration in Hungary by force and it was left to Bánffy and his Prime Minister, István Bethlen, to defuse an explosive situation. King Charles was formally obliged to abdicate and Bánffy's role in the affair earned him the enmity of the legitimists. He was also to receive criticism from an unexpected quarter: Mihály Károlyi's wife, Katinka Andrássy, wrote that Bánffy was 'More adept at upholstering the royal throne than in upholding it', a spiteful remark and a cheeky one, coming from the wife of a man who had dethroned the same King Charles only three years earlier.

Bánffy's lasting achievement as Foreign Minister was the settling of the dispute over the Burgenland, a strip of western Hungarian territory assigned to Austria at the Paris Peace Conference but still in the possession of armed Hungarian irregulars. It was now that his Italian friendships proved useful. He and Bethlen accepted an Italian mediation offer and met the Austrians in Venice. After lengthy negotiations, the Austrians agreed to a plebiscite, as a result of which the city of Sopron remained in Hungary and the rest of the Burgenland was handed over to the Austrians. It was to be the only breach in the harsh provisions of the Treaty of

Trianon, the same treaty which had assigned Transylvania—and thus Kolozsvár (Cluj-Napoca), Bonchida (Bonțida) and Gyalu (Gilău)—to Romania.

Four years later, Bánffy returned to Transylvania to find the situation there radically changed. Romanian land reform—though it provided for some compensation—had deprived the family of much of its land. Bánffy used what was left of his fortune to subsidise Hungarian-language newspapers and journals as well as to help writers in need, but his presence was not universally welcomed by Hungarian politicians in Transylvania. Many felt that he was too eager to establish links with the new rulers and that he had too many friends among Romanian intellectuals. For the remainder of his career he tried to steer clear of divisive and increasingly radical politics. When Hitler installed the Hungarian Nazi, Szálasi, as 'Leader of the Nation' in October 1944 (when parts of Transylvania were briefly Hungarian again following the Vienna Award), Bánffy resigned his seat in the Hungarian Upper House.

Meanwhile, his personal life had undergone a major transformation. In 1939, at the age of sixty-five, he decided to get married. His bride was the distinguished actress Aranka Váradi, to whom he had been linked by strong ties of affection for decades and with whom he had a daughter. This marriage would not have been possible during his father's lifetime but since the latter had died ten years earlier, the way was now free. His daughter, Katalin (henceforth Bánffy), would devote her later life to translating the *Transylvanian Trilogy* into English. Without her efforts, her father's work would not enjoy the international reputation it does today.

Bánffy, together with his wife and daughter, spent the Soviet siege of Budapest at his family house in Reviczky Street. As soon it was possible, in early 1945, they left for Kolozsvár. They found the city under Soviet occupation and the sight of devastated, burnt and pillaged Bonchida, a few days later, was a mortal blow. And though Miklós Bánffy's return was initially welcomed by the locals, Communist and nationalist agitators did their best to make things difficult. Villagers were told to ignore 'the old tyrant'.

After a few weeks in Transylvania, Aranka and Katalin decided to return to Budapest. Bánffy would never see his daughter again. Passports to leave Romania were almost impossible to obtain. Attempts to publish his most recent works were stopped by a series of increasingly hostile attacks in the Press. Though deprived of his livelihood, he continued to write. 'Were I unable to write,' he told Katinka, 'I would go stark raving mad.' And yet in the midst of his increasing misery, he wrote lighthearted pieces, humorous comedies. 'The worse off one is, the better one seems to be able to write humorously,' he wrote to his daughter. 'When I lived well, I wrote nothing but dramas.'

His financial position was becoming daily more untenable and his house in Kolozsvár was occupied by squatters, whose presence was sanctioned by the new authorities. One of the squatters took pity on him and allowed him to occupy one barely heated room on the ground floor. This is where visitors saw him, sitting in a worn armchair in threadbare clothes, surrounded by a few remnants of former glory: a couple of inlaid Baroque chests laden down with books and manuscripts, all covered with a generous coating of dust. But he was to be deprived even of this modest refuge. In the summer of 1949, his house was formally confiscated. As he wrote to his sister: 'They not only took the house but have ordered me to leave at once.' The desperation emanating from his letter to prime minister Petru Groza requesting a passport—yet again—to leave the country makes for difficult reading, even at a distance of more than seventy years. 'I have lost my entire fortune and not having a pension, now, at the age of seventy-six, in the strictest meaning of the word, I have nothing from which to live...I have no choice but to commit suicide or die of starvation...'

At last, in the autumn of 1949, the passport arrived. 'It is painful for me to leave everything behind,' Bánffy told Katinka. 'Kolozsvár, our old house, Házsongárd cemetery where our loved ones lie, thousands and thousands of memories. It is awful, but there is no other way.' On 15th of October, five years almost to the day after the destruction of Bonchida, he boarded a train for Budapest. The historian Lajos Kelemen wrote without an ounce of compassion that he had just gone to see off someone who once was the heir to the largest fortune in Transylvania but was now reduced to the status of a beggar. When Bánffy arrived in Budapest, his wife was shocked by his appearance: 'Clothed in rags, thin and greatly aged; a weak, old man with almost trembling legs. He hasn't got a shirt or a pair of trousers—but oh, how joyful it is that he should be finally here!'

Aranka Bánffy's joy was to be short-lived. Her husband died some eight months after his arrival, on 6th June 1950. His funeral was a simple affair. Two elderly women followed the coffin, his wife and sister. His daughter, living in Morocco, could not attend, nor could his nephew: neither would have been allowed into the country. Official Hungary ignored the event; the Communist terror was just switching into full gear. Even people who would have wanted to come were frightened to do so. Despite this, a few brave souls from the Opera appeared with a wreath bought at their own expense.

The Calvinist bishop László Ravasz—himself in the sights of the dreaded secret police—came to deliver Bánffy's eulogy. 'Where is his wealth now?' he asked with a rhetorical flourish. 'Where is his talent, his social position, his seemingly indestructible good health? Nothing is left but Jesus.' The bishop was wrong. Everything else may have turned to dust and ashes but the talent remained and is with us still.

Thomas Barcsay. Toronto, 2021

Published in Hungary
Felelős kiadó a Somerset Kiadó és Tanácsadó Kft. ügyvezető igazgatója
1136 Budapest, Pannónia u. 11.
Szerkesztő: Annabel Barber
Nyomdai előkészítés: Kuzmich Anikó
Nyomta és kötötte TJ Books, Anglia
ISBN 978-1-905131-89-1